# A LONG GOOD-BYE

Piers had come to bid her farewell. For his friendly visits to Alice had to end, now that he was pledged to wed the adorable and innocent Miss Cassandra Borden.

His hands tightened on hers. "It is always hard to say good-bye, is it not?" he said, leaning forward to kiss her on the cheek.

"Yes," Alice said, "always hard. Good-bye, then, Piers." She smiled through the tears in her eyes. And she stretched up to kiss him softly on the cheek.

"Allie," he said, and bent his head and kissed her briefly and softly on the lips. He looked questioningly into her eyes.

This, she knew, was the time to draw away . . . before the love she could no longer deny led to a folly she could not resist . . .

MARY BALOGH was raised and educated in Wales, and now lives in Kipling, Saskatchewan, Canada, with her husband, Robert, and her children, Jacqueline, Christopher, and Sian. She is a high school English teacher.

# SIGNET REGENCY ROMANCE
## COMING IN MARCH 1991

### *Anita Mills*
Miss Gordon's Mistake

### *Michele Kasey*
The Somerville Farce

### *Margaret Westhaven*
The Duke's Design

# A CERTAIN MAGIC

## by Mary Balogh

A SIGNET BOOK

SIGNET
Published by the Penguin Group
Penguin Books USA Inc., 375 Hudson Street,
New York, New York 10014, U.S.A.
Penguin Books Ltd, 27 Wrights Lane,
London W8 5TZ, England
Penguin Books Australia Ltd, Ringwood,
Victoria, Australia
Penguin Books Canada Ltd, 2801 John Street,
Markham, Ontario, Canada L3R 1B4
Penguin Books (N.Z.) Ltd, 182-190 Wairau Road,
Auckland 10, New Zealand

Penguin Books Ltd, Registered Offices:
Harmondsworth, Middlesex, England

First published by Signet, an imprint of New American Library, a division
of Penguin Books USA Inc.

First Printing, February, 1991
10  9  8  7  6  5  4  3  2  1

*For Maryann again
with many thanks
for the basic story idea*

# 1

WHEN a plain but elegant town carriage drew up outside Number Eight, Portman Square, late on the morning of a cloudy April day, it was obvious that it was expected. The doors of the house opened immediately, and a manservant descended the steps in order to throw back the door of the carriage and set down the steps.

A gentleman of early middle years, dressed with impeccable correctness for morning, hovered inside the doorway, but would not demean himself by stepping outside onto the steps. He clasped his hands behind him and frowned. From the lines on his forehead and the creases that ran from his sharp nose to his chin, it appeared that such an expression was not uncommon with him.

A lady set a gloved hand in that of the manservant and accepted his assistance to descend the steps. She smiled at him.

"Thank you, Muggins," she said. "And how do you do? You have recovered from your attack of gout? I trust Mrs. Muggins is well?"

She smoothed out the folds of her elegant carriage dress as she continued to smile. She listened to the servant's reply as if she had a genuine interest in his words.

"And pleased I am to see you, Mrs. Penhallow, ma'am," Muggins made so bold as to add, "and pleased Mrs. Muggins will be, too."

"Muggins!" the gentleman called from inside the doorway. "You will not keep my sister talking on the public street, if you please."

The lady looked toward the doorway and smiled afresh. She walked quickly up the steps, both hands held out before her. She was considerably younger than her brother—no girl, it was true, but not yet approaching middle years. Her large, soft dark eyes and good-humored mouth suggested that she was unlike him in other ways, as well.

"Bruce," she said, taking his hands in both of hers and turning her cheek for his kiss. "I came as soon as I read your letter."

"The mails are not what they used to be," he grumbled. "I wrote four days ago. I shall stay here and see that Muggins and your coachman lift down your baggage carefully. It would be too mortifying if they set some of it down on the pavement for all the world to see, as they are sure to do if they think I am not watching."

"But I am staying in Cavendish Square," she said. "I arrived yesterday, too late to call here. Had you forgotten that Web had a house in town?"

Her brother frowned as he turned from the door. "Not staying here?" he said. "When I wrote to tell you particularly that Phoebe has need of you? You will just have to move your baggage here today, Alice. There is no point in keeping two establishments open in town, anyway. A dreadful waste of money. I shall arrange it."

"You must not provoke yourself," Mrs. Alice Penhallow said briskly, removing her bonnet and kid gloves. "You forget that Web left me a comfortable fortune along with the house, Bruce. And as for Phoebe having need of me, that is why I have come. I am entirely at her disposal during the days. I shall spend the nights in my own home. How are the children?"

"Spotty," he said, "and feverish. And peevish. Amanda is to be kept away from them for fear that she will take the infection and not be able to continue with her come-out after all. Imagine what a waste of money that would prove to be after I have taken this house and removed my whole family here for the Season at considerable expense. And Jarvis arrived four days ago—just one hour after I sent a letter on the way to you—sent down from Oxford, though it was on an utterly unjust charge, as I shall explain to someone in no uncertain terms when Phoebe has calmed down and I can see to my own affairs again.''

Alice took his arm and patted it soothingly. ''Poor Phoebe must be hagged,'' she said. ''I shall help her with the nursing of the children, and she will be as cheerful as ever in no time at all, you will see. Now, are we to stand in the hallway all morning, or is there somewhere else we should go?''

''Mrs. Muggins was instructed to bring tea to the morning room,'' he said, leading the way to the stairs. His tone was aggrieved. ''But if you completed your journey yesterday, Alice, and have merely driven from Cavendish Square this morning, then I daresay you have had tea already.''

''With my breakfast,'' she said. ''Three hours ago. Another cup now will be very welcome, Bruce. Persuade Phoebe to join me, do. She will be able to tell me exactly what the state of affairs in the sickroom is so that I will be able to make an intelligent contribution as a nurse for the rest of the day.''

''Have you had the measles?'' he asked. ''I was not at all sure. You had better not go into the nursery if you have not, you know, for measles can be fatal to an adult, so I have heard.''

Alice laughed. ''When I was a child,'' she said. ''Go and fetch Phoebe.''

She expected to find her sister-in-law on the verge of nervous collapse after the ordeals of the past week, during which her two younger children had come down with measles. Phoebe had always liked to view herself as a woman of frail constitution from as far back as Alice could remember. But the agitated manner and abstracted air with which she greeted the new arrival in the morning room had another cause.

It seemed that the sick children were not the mother's chief worry. Her main concern was that she would be neither available nor in the best spirits to shepherd her daughter around to the dizzying number of balls and routs and concerts that a young lady making her come-out was expected to attend.

"For I must make the sacrifice, like it or not, Alice," she explained fretfully, leaning forward in her chair and speaking in her usual breathless voice, as if she were confiding the most scandalous of secrets. "Even if my poor darlings are at death's door, I must sacrifice my maternal instincts for my dearest Amanda. She must not be the last of the young ladies on the dangle for husbands this year to find one. Imagine the disgrace to your brother, Alice."

Alice understood perfectly why she had been summoned. Not that she had been in any doubt from the moment she had broken the seal on her brother's letter when it arrived in Bath. She had sighed then and sat down to pen her regrets to several friends who were expecting her company at various entertainments over the coming weeks. And she had known, as she set her maid to packing her trunks for a stay of a few weeks in London, that she must not expect any social pleasures to attach themselves to her stay.

Only one self-indulgence she would insist on, she had decided. She would stay in her own house. It would be a haven of sanity to which she could retire every evening. Being nine-and-twenty years old and a widow of somewhat more than comfortable means had its definite advantages even though she had not for one moment wished poor Web in his grave during the nine years of their marriage.

"Lady Jersey herself smiled most graciously at Amanda two evenings ago at Lord Maitland's ball," Phoebe was saying. "I would not be surprised at all, Alice, to find that we will have vouchers for Almack's before the month is out."

"Whom did you bring with you as a companion?" Bruce asked, his voice an accusation. "And never tell me you brought that Mrs. Potter, Alice. Her husband used to be in business.''

"And needs her presence in Bath far more than I need it here," Alice said soothingly. "I brought my maid with me—Penelope, you know. And very excited she is, too, to be in London. She could scarce keep her nose from touching the glass of the window as we drove to Cavendish Square. But I brought no companion, Bruce. I do not need one."

"Oh, my dear," her sister-in-law said, shocked. "You cannot stay alone in London. It is not done."

"It is, by me," Alice said, setting down her cup and saucer on the table beside her.

"You do not care at all what people may say about my allowing such scandalous behavior in my sister, I suppose," Bruce said irritably.

"Not at all," Alice agreed.

"Mr. Westhaven danced the opening set of country dances with Amanda at the Maitland ball," Phoebe said. "We were very obliged to him, Alice. He quite brought her into fashion. Her card filled up with no trouble at all once he was seen to lead her out."

"Piers?" Alice said. "At a ball? How funny. I cannot quite imagine Piers at anything so formal. He is still in town, then?"

"Oh, yes," her sister-in-law said, leaning so far forward she was almost out of her chair, "and will be for the Season, I daresay. They say he is dangling after a wife, Alice. And high time, too, him being heir now to Lord Berringer of Bingamen Hall in Bedfordshire. It is only right that he take another wife. He has worn the willow for poor Mrs. Westhaven for almost nine years. The thought has crossed my mind that perhaps he fancies dear Amanda, but I think he is perhaps a little old. Do you?"

"Piers?" Alice said. "And Amanda? Oh, yes, Phoebe, I think he is certainly too old. Amanda is barely eighteen. Piers is thirty-six."

"Of course," her sister-in-law said, her eyes thoughtful, "it would be a splendid match for her.

Everyone is wondering whom he will choose. It would be a great coup for your brother if we could land Mr. Westhaven.''

Alice stood up. "It is time I saw Richard and Mary," she said, "since it was for their sakes I came. Take me to them, Phoebe. If they have been sick for a week, I suppose they are on the mend already, are they?"

"Oh, dear, no," their fond mother assured her. "Mary favors me, you know. She is very delicate. Dr. Plaidy feared for her life and still pays daily visits to her bedside. And Dickie's fever will not come down if you cannot keep him quiet, Alice, especially now that Jarvis is home. Dickie worships Jarvis, you know."

Alice ascended the stairs behind her sister-in-law, resigned to a day spent in a stuffy sickroom with two peevish patients.

Piers, she thought. Piers and Amanda. Oh, no, never in a million Sundays. He would devour the poor girl for breakfast.

Piers attending London balls during the Season? And dancing? Piers looking around him for a new bride?

She shook off the strange images that the thoughts aroused and smiled as Phoebe opened the door into the darkened nursery.

Alice was writing a letter the following morning in the small library that her husband had used as his study whenever they were in town. She was informing Andrea Potter that the situation at Portman Square was not by any means as desperate as it had been made to seem in her brother's letter. Mary merely needed someone to sit with her and sympathize with her and listen to her complaints. Richard, though still spotty, was roaring back to health and merely needed activity.

The day before, after Phoebe had taken Amanda on an afternoon of visiting, and Bruce, in great relief, had taken himself off to one of his clubs, she had pulled back some of the heavy curtains in the nursery and even opened a window despite Mary's complaints and Richard's sniggering claim that his mama would have the vapors. And having ascertained from the doctor that neither child was any longer infectious and from Jarvis that he had had the measles years before anyway, she had allowed the older brother to visit the younger on condition that he did not entertain Richard with all the details of the escapade that had resulted in his being sent down from Oxford.

He had told her, with great enthusiasm and righteous indignation at the harshness of the punishment, that he and three cronies had smuggled two females of doubtful virtue into their dormitory and been caught when one of the females had proved to be an inveterate giggler. All four young men had been sent down for the rest of the year.

Alice did not confide any of those details to her Bath friend. She folded the letter and got to her feet, intending to order the carriage to take her to Portman Square for the rest of the day. But a brief tap on the door forestalled her. She looked up to find, not her manservant bowing with deference before divulging his message, but a cheerfully smiling London gentleman.

He was fashionably dressed, from the slightly disheveled cut of his fair hair to the white tassels on his Hessian boots. Yet he wore his clothes with an easy, almost careless air. He appeared equally unabsorbed by his tall, muscular frame and handsome face. He was a gentleman past his youth and yet clearly in his prime. He had opened the door himself and entered the library unannounced.

"Allie!" he said, coming purposefully toward her with outstretched arms. "Why did you not write to say you were coming?" He enfolded her in a hearty hug and kissed her on the cheek before releasing her.

"Piers," she said, laughing up at him. "Looking the complete town gentleman."

He held his arms out to the sides and looked down at himself in some amusement. "Splendid, am I not?"

he said. "But do you not think the haircut the coup de grace, Allie? I was persuaded that I would be quite top-of-the-trees with it styled this way. It is called a Brutus, by the way. And before you think to frown and wonder why I do not comb it more neatly, I beg leave to inform you that it is meant to be disheveled. It is fashionable thus."

She laughed again. "I am rendered quite speechless with admiration," she said.

"And so you should be." He took both her hands in his own and squeezed them. "Why did you not write to me?"

"I came away in a hurry," she said. "Bruce wrote, and nothing would do but I must come immediately or sooner if at all possible. Besides, you have your own life and do not need to be forever at my beck and call."

"What?" he said. "I am supposed to show no interest at all when my dearest friend comes to town? Shall we sit?"

"For a few minutes," she said, taking a wing chair facing into the room and watching him settle his long limbs into a chair beside her. "I promised to be in Portman Square before luncheon."

"The children are ill," he said. "Your sister-in-law told me so several days ago, though she did not mention that Bruce had sent for you. And so you have been summoned as nurse because a mother and father and older sister and brother and a houseful of servants including a nurse employed for the job are not enough. Allie, you are being put upon again."

"Never say so," she said with a smile. "What else are single aunts for?"

"For getting on with their own lives, that is what," he said. "I was coming down to Bath to visit you after Christmas, you know, but those infernal relatives of mine decided to get themselves killed both together and catapulted me into the dizzying position of being heir to a bona fide baron. I had to go into Bedfordshire to pay homage to his lordship instead of going to Bath.''

"Piers!'' she said, laughing despite herself. "Those poor young men. And they were your relatives. Have you no feeling at all for their deaths? And you are not wearing mourning?''

"Good Lord, no,'' he said. "They were nothing to me, Allie. I never saw them in my life, and they were very distant relatives, you know. Dozens of seconds and thirds and removes involved in the relationship. They were not even the direct descendants of the present Lord Berringer, merely a little more closely related than I. A few less removes, I gather. There are enough occasions in life when one must grieve. One does not need to take the burdens of the world on one's shoulders.''

"So,'' Alice said, "I may one day expect to have to address you as 'my lord,' may I?''

"The devil!'' he said. "Don't you ever dare, my girl. How is Bath treating you? You are looking very fine and not at all provincial.''

"It suits me,'' she said. "It must be the most beautiful city in England, Piers.''

"Granted,'' he said. "But full of octogenarians, I hear. I don't at all like the thought of your living there. I suppose you have dozens of aged and retired generals and whatnot ogling you and wanting to hire you on as nursemaid for their old age at the cost of a marriage license.''

Alice was laughing. "Oh, not dozens,'' she said. "You exaggerate. No more than half a dozen.''

"Well,'' he said, "I wish you had not left home, Allie. I have no reason to spend time at Westhaven Park any longer. First Web dying two years ago and then you purchasing a house in Bath last summer and taking yourself off. It's deuced lonely at home without either of you.''

"Is it?'' she said. "But I did not have a great deal of choice once Web's cousin decided last year to move into Chandlos after all. The house belonged to him.

And I am not complaining. It was the only one of Web's possessions that did not come to me, and he would have left me that, too, if he could. Oh, I could have taken a house in the village, Piers, but I did not think it fair to stay in the neighborhood. There are those who would have said I had been forced from my own home, and that would not have been fair at all. It was better to move right away.''

"But it *was* your home," he said, "all your life. Oh, not Chandlos until you married Web, but the village. Your father was rector there even before you were born.''

"Yes," she said. "But I had to leave, Piers. There was no one left—Papa gone, Web gone, y—. Well." She smiled. "It was better to begin a new life altogether. How did you know I was here?''

"Met your sister-in-law at the opera last evening," he said. "I'm sorry, Allie. Have I upset you, reminding you of Web?''

"No, not at all," she said. "After two years I can both think of him and speak of him without dissolving into the vapors, you know.''

"You did from the start," he said. "You never did collapse. Only your eyes showed what was going on inside. Well, he was a damned fool for going out shooting in the rain when he was still recovering from the influenza, and I would have told him so, too, if I had been home at the time. I would have wrestled him back into his bed for you, Allie. Anyway, enough of that. You would never guess what is going on in my life.''

"Perhaps I could, too," she said. "I have been hearing strange things of you, Piers. You have been attending balls and dancing, too, which is a very strange combination indeed. And attending the opera last evening? And of course, there are the elegant clothes and the, ah, Brutus hairdo. I think perhaps you are losing your grip on your sanity.''

He threw back his head and shouted with laughter. "Perhaps I am, too," he said. "Though if you were to talk to Mama, she would tell you that I am just being restored to my senses after a very long time. For apparently I have been in a long decline since Harriet's death, from which sad fate only my recent promotion to Berringer's heir has awakened me. I am looking for a leg-shackle, Allie. I am looking to be a tenant-for-life again. Though I was not quite that the first time as it turned out, was I? Poor Harriet. It lasted less than two years.''

"Surely you cannot be as careless about the matter as you appear to be," Alice said. "Have you met the lady, Piers? And can you like her and even love her?''

"Romantic Allie," he said, chuckling. "Oh, no, my dear, not all marriages can be as perfect as yours was, you know. You and Web were companions and lovers. It is a rare combination, I would have you know, my fair innocent. I do not see many such marriages around me. My own was not by any means ideal, though Harriet was quite blameless and I was fond of her. Marriages when you are about to be catapulted into the nobility are definitely not made in heaven.''

"Oh," she said, "you cannot be so cynical, Piers. You would hate a marriage that did not bring you companionship.''

"Would I?" he said, his eyes twinkling at her. "I think not. It seems I need a breeder. Don't look so shocked, Allie—you are not a miss from the schoolroom. I need a dozen sons so that Bingamen Hall will be in no danger of reverting to someone with even more removes to his relationship than mine.''

"As if you cared for titles and property," she said scornfully. "You have Westhaven Park and a vast fortune besides.''

He laughed. "But one becomes public property when one is in danger of taking on a title," he said. "At least, one becomes one's mama's property. She is vastly impressed with my new status, Allie, and quite insistent that I give up my widowed state. I will have to choose a sweet young thing, someone who can breed for me for the next twenty years or so. I am bound to find someone this spring. The city is positively bursting at the seams with them.''

"Piers!" Alice scolded.

"Oh, have no fear," he said. "I shall treat her well, Allie, once I have made her Mrs. Westhaven with the carrot of becoming Lady Berringer dangling in front of her nose. I always treated Harriet well.''

"Yes, you did," she agreed.

He uncrossed his ankles and stood up abruptly. "Apart from the small matter that I killed her," he said.

Alice rose, too, and set a hand on his arm. "No," she said. "I thought you had long ago put such a nonsensical idea behind you. Of course you did not kill her. Many women die in childbed, Piers. It is a fact of our existence.''

"Well," he said. "It was my child that killed her, was it not? I was not aware that she was sleeping with anyone else.''

"Nonsense!" she said. "You must not start doing this again. Web is no longer here to deal with you. Is it because you are thinking of marrying again? And having children again?''

He laughed. "When I have a dozen sons and half a dozen daughters," he said, "will you come and nurse them when they fall sick with measles or influenza or ill-nature, Allie?''

"Goodness," she said, horrified. "Of course I will not. I will not be their aunt and will owe them no attention at all.''

"No, you won't, will you?" he said regretfully. "But if I fall sick of bad temper from having so many bawling infants around me, will you come and nurse me, Allie?''

"Not at all," she said. "You will have a wife to perform that office. I shall merely write you a letter to tell you that it serves you right.''

"Will you?" he said. "How unkind of you. You need not order your carriage, Allie. I brought the curricle, guessing that you would be on your way to Portman Square. I will drive you there as soon as you have put on your bonnet. You must not let Bruce and your sister-in-law or those children monopolize your time, by the way. I demand some of it. I shall take you to the theater and drive you about London. I need some sensible companionship occasionally.''

"If you wish to impress some sweet young thing," she said, "you will not wish to be seen with me."

"Oh, you are quite out there," he said. "They are already falling all over themselves, you know, not to mention their mamas. It would quite go to my head, Allie, if the same females had not almost ignored me just five months ago."

"I shall fetch my bonnet," Alice said.

# 2

DURING the afternoon of the same day in another part of London, a post-chaise was setting down two weary travelers outside a handsome town house on Russell Square. Though two servants hurried immediately down the steps in order to unload their baggage and carry it inside, the master of this house did not stand on ceremony or think it beneath his dignity to run down the steps himself, despite his considerable bulk, in order to catch up first one of the female travelers in his arms and then the other. He kissed both loudly and was seen to be beaming with goodwill.

"Lucinda!" he said to the older lady. "Come on inside and have some tea and cakes. There is nothing to wear one down more, is there, than two nights spent at inns. Did you bring your own bed linen as I advised you to do?" But he turned to the younger lady without waiting for an answer. "Cassie!" he said. "Looking as fine as fivepence and good enough to eat. Come to town looking for a husband, have you? Trust your uncle to find you the finest one to be had."

"Brother!" the elder lady said, taking his arm in a determined hold and drawing him in the direction of the front door. "The tea will be very welcome, though Cassandra should avoid the cakes. We were forced to spend three nights on the road because of the rain."

The Honorable Miss Cassandra Borden followed her mother and her uncle into the house.

"So," Mr. Bosley said as soon as servants had handed around tea and cakes and withdrawn from the drawing room. He smiled fondly at his niece. "Getting ready to take the town by storm, are you, Cassie? You are quite pretty enough to turn all the right heads even as you are. By the time I have decked you out in all the most expensive finery, there won't be a prince in England not on his knees to you." He laughed merrily.

"Oh, Uncle!" the girl said, blushing and staring into her cup.

"We don't necessarily want a prince," Lady Margam said briskly. "But living in the country with Margam gone and not a feather to fly with is not finding Cassandra any husband at all. We want someone respectable and well set up."

"When she is the daughter of Lord Margam and niece of one of the wealthiest merchants in London?" Mr. Bosley said, looking at his sister in some surprise. "Come, come, Lucinda, we can do a great deal better than that. You would like something better than a respectable husband, wouldn't you now, Cassie? Eh?"

"If you please, Uncle," she said, not looking up from her teacup.

"As pretty as a picture," Mr. Bosley said, gazing with genial fondness at his niece. "You did well by yourself, Lucinda. You can gain entrance to all the most tonnish affairs with no trouble at all. All you need is some of my money to set you and the girl up, and there is plenty of that. After all, you are my only sister and Cassie is my only niece. What else are family for?"

"I am much obliged, brother," Lady Margam said. "But Margam was never one to spend a great deal of time in town. I do not know how we are to be in receipt of any invitations, I am sure."

"I have connections," Mr. Bosley said. "There are people who owe me favors." He chuckled merrily. "And money, too. I can get the girl taken on. But is there no one you know, Lucinda? It would be so much better if you could gain entry into society on your own account."

"No one," she said. "There was only Lady Henley,

Margam's aunt, who is now deceased, may God rest her soul. And Mr. Trentley, his cousin, who is in America, if I do not mistake the matter. And Mr. Westhaven, his particular friend at Cambridge, who may be deceased, too, for all I know.''

"No, he is not, though,'' Mr. Bosley said. "Westhaven? Heir to Lord Berringer? He is in town and much sought after, too. I have been sniffing around me for the last month or so, since I knew Cassie would be coming to find herself a husband. Westhaven is on the lookout for a wife.''

"He was Margam's particular friend,'' Lady Margam said. "When we were first married and living in Cambridge, that was.''

"Then you must renew the acquaintance,'' Mr. Bosley said, beaming. "He will escort you to some grand do, Lucinda, and Cassie too, of course. He will bring her into fashion. This could not be more fortunate.'' He rubbed his large hands together with satisfaction.

"But I have not seen him in fifteen years,'' Lady Margam said. "Cassandra was a mere baby. Though Margam saw him after that, once or twice.''

"You shall send him an invitation to tea,'' Mr. Bosley said. "It will be perfectly acceptable for you to invite him to your brother's house, will it not? Even if it is a merchant's house?''

"I don't know, I am sure,'' she said doubtfully.

"He can do wonders for Cassie,'' her brother said.

"Mama?'' The girl looked up at her mother with large green eyes. "Will I be going to balls soon?''

"Oh, yes, soon, my love,'' her mother said. "As soon as Uncle has outfitted you with all you will need. I suppose I should write to Mr. Westhaven, though I daresay he will consider it most strange. He used to be an excessively handsome and amiable young man, to be sure.''

"There is every chance that he will fall for Cassie,'' her uncle said. "And why should he not? She is young and pretty and the daughter of nobility—on the one side, anyway. And the daughter of his friend, to boot. I shall let it be known, you may be sure, Lucinda, what dowry I am prepared to give with my only niece. Many gentlemen of the *ton* will find themselves unable to resist that lure, I do assure you. Expensive creatures, every last one of them. Perhaps we will have a husband for you almost before we start, Cassie. How would you like that, girl?''

"Oh, Uncle!'' she said, blushing and gazing down into her empty teacup.

"She likes it, you see?'' Mr. Bosley said, beaming at his sister. "Mrs. Westhaven. In time to be lady Berringer of Bingamen Hall in Bedfordshire. It sounds fine indeed, don't it, though? Fine, anyway, to an uncle who made his fortune in fish.'' He laughed heartily and sipped noisily at his almost cold tea.

Amanda Carpenter had been invited to join a party of new acquaintances on a visit to the Tower two days later. The group was to be well chaperoned. Her presence would not be necessary, Phoebe announced to Alice the evening before, when she and her daughter finally returned from a soirée.

"And glad I am of it,'' she said with a sigh, kicking off her evening slippers and sinking onto a sofa. "You can be very thankful you are not a mother, Alice. For no sooner have you finished with nursing and teething and worrying about them falling into streams or down stairs but you must concern yourself with their education and worry that they will turn out to be perfect dunderheads. And no sooner is that all over with but you must start to think about marrying them off as well as may be.''

"Amanda seems to be taking very well,'' Alice said soothingly, rising from her chair and folding her embroidery. She would be glad to get home. The children had been asleep for a few hours, but there was no place to relax properly but in one's own home.

"Her father will be besieged with offers before many weeks have passed, to be sure,'' Phoebe said. "And thankful I am that that it is his responsibility to choose wisely and not mine, Alice. It really does not seem fair that all the responsibility for the well-being of children falls on a mother's shoulders, does it?''

No answer seemed to be called for. Alice made none, but placed her embroidery neatly inside her work bag.

''Tending the children on their sickbeds all day and running after Amanda all night is quite wearing out my nerves,'' her sister-in-law said. ''I am sure you are in good looks, Alice, and glad I am for you. It is unfortunate that you have no husband or child, but you must count your blessings. You do not have a mother's worries, either.''

Alice smiled, kissed Phoebe on the cheek, and took her leave. She sank back against the cushions of her carriage a few minutes later and looked forward to an unexpected free day on the morrow. Although Phoebe had hinted that she was hagged enough to rest for the whole day if her sister-in-law would just be good enough to come and sit in the sickroom during the afternoon, Alice had resisted. She would sit with the children during the evening, she had promised, when Phoebe would be called upon to accompany Amanda to a rout.

She resisted the urge to feel irritated with her sister-in-law. After all, Phoebe had always been the same, even before she had married Bruce, and certainly before she had had her children. Always self-centered and quite tactless.

Yes, she was fortunate indeed to be without husband or child, she thought, closing her eyes rather wearily. Did Phoebe have any conception of the vast emptiness that life was capable of offering? she wondered. Doubtless not.

Web had been part of her life since she was a girl. They were older than she, both Web and Piers—Piers by seven years and Web by eight. She had thought them both very dashing as she grew past childhood. She had known as soon as she reached a girl's awareness of such matters—when she was fifteen—that Web loved her, just as surely as she knew that Piers did not.

Web had asked her father for her when she was approaching her eighteenth birthday, and she had agreed to marry him. She had liked him, though he had never been a handsome man. His figure was a little too much on the portly side, his sandy hair was a little too thin, and his face a little too round for classic good looks. But his face had always been kindly and good-humored. She had agreed to marry him because she liked him and because she wanted to spend the rest of her life where she had grown up, though her grandfather probably would have given her a Season if she had asked Papa to write to him, just as he had educated Bruce from the age of twelve and given him a home, too.

She had married Web because she was willing to settle for contentment and because even at the age of seventeen she had been a realist. Life could never offer what she most dreamed of.

She had married Web determined to make his happiness the goal of her life. And she thought she had succeeded. He had never stopped worshiping her until the day of his death. And she had been well rewarded for her devotion to him. She had grown dearly fond of him. So much so that her life had collapsed about her for a full year after his death. Despite what Piers had said just the day before, she had collapsed inwardly. She had not known how to live without Web.

And oh, yes, she thought, her mind flashing back to Phoebe for a moment, she was fortunate indeed to be without the burden of children. Sometimes she really thought that Phoebe must have forgotten. Or how could she be so cruel?

Nicholas, with his father's chubbiness and sweet smile and her own very dark hair and eyes. Well, she thought, it was probably easy for Phoebe to forget. She had never seen the child, and he had been less than a year old when Web had found him dead in his crib one afternoon. There had been no detectable cause of death.

He would be ten years old now. Doubtless into all kinds of mischief. She was fortunate to have been saved the trouble.

Web had been unwilling to get her with child again. He had been inconsolable for many months and unwilling to risk that kind of love again. He had been unwilling to risk her life again, especially after Harriet Westhaven had died in childbed less than a year later.

Piers had been so distraught that both she and Web had feared that he might put an end to his own life.

Yes, she must be thankful, Alice thought, setting her head back against the cushions and keeping her eyes closed. In all seriousness, she must be thankful. She had lived a good life, and now she had the means with which to do what she pleased and make the remainder of her life as comfortable as possible.

She had a visitor the following morning. She smiled with some amusement as she rose from her desk, where she was again writing a letter. He had decided to be more proper this morning and send her servant to announce him. Her spirits lifted unconsciously.

But it was not Piers Westhaven who walked through the doorway, but another familiar figure.

"Sir Clayton!" she said, extending one hand and moving toward him. "What a very pleasant surprise. What brings you to London?"

"A need for a change of scenery, Mrs. Penhallow," he said, taking her hand and raising it to his lips. "And you, of course."

Alice smiled and retrieved her hand as soon as she could do so without snatching it. How very tiresome! Sir Clayton Lansing, long-time resident of Bath, had been markedly attentive almost from the moment of her arrival there the summer before. She could not go to the Pump Room without having to promenade around it at least once with him. She could not take tea at the Upper Rooms without having to share a table with him. She could not shop on Milsom Street without having to relinquish her parcels to him to carry home for her.

Oh, dear!

"How very flattering, sir," she said. "And what a bouncer. It is April and the time of the Season, and reason enough for anyone to come to town. You are staying with your sister?"

"I am," he said. "And I trust your nephew and niece are out of danger, ma'am? Mrs. Potter informed me that they were dangerously ill. I was very distressed."

"They have the measles," Alice said. "Or had them, rather. They are recovering quite nicely, I thank you."

She rang for tea and was thankful that Sir Clayton was at least punctilious in his social manners. He would not stay beyond half an hour.

He did not, but he did ask her, as he kissed her hand on taking his leave, if she would do him the honor of joining him at the theater one evening when he could get up a party.

"If it is possible, sir," she said, her tone regretful. "Though it is during the evenings, you know, that my sister-in-law needs me most, her time being given to my elder niece, who is making her come out."

No engagement was made as Sir Clayton bowed himself out. He was to drop her a note when he could make more definite plans.

One had to be quite firm and quite rude with the man, Andrea Potter had told her with a laugh several months before. There was no way by which persons of Sir Clayton's obtuseness could be put off with gentle hints.

"Unless you like him, of course, Alice," her friend had said, "or could be brought to like him. He is enormously wealthy, by all accounts. And he cannot be above twenty years your senior. Indeed, it sounds quite like a match made in heaven."

Alice had given her giggling friend a speaking glance, but had not deigned to reply.

Sometimes, she thought now, one could be almost thankful for relatives sick with the measles. Measles were indisputable. She would find it very difficult to say an outright no if she did not have a ready-made excuse. Sir Clayton Lansing was so very worthy and respectable.

Alice was coming out of a milliner's shop on Oxford Street a few hours later, a hatbox dangling from a ribbon in her hand. She had only rarely had a chance to shop in London. Web and she had not come often despite the fact that he had always owned the house on Cavendish Square. As often as not he had had it rented out.

But today was a fine April day and and she was feeling free and frivolous.

"A quite delightful and decidedly wicked smile," a careless voice said almost at her shoulder. "It is my guess that you have been spending a fortune on a new bonnet that you do not at all need. And that you are not even the smallest bit contrite."

"Piers," she said, turning toward him with a dazzling smile. "You are quite right, of course. It is a thoroughly foolish confection that I shall not have the temerity to wear in Bath."

"Then you must wear it in London," he said. "I shall take you driving in Hyde Park one afternoon. At five o'clock, of course—it must be at the fashionable hour. And all the gentlemen will be smitten from the backs of their horses, and all the ladies' eyes will turn collectively green."

She laughed.

"They will, you know," he said. "You have no business still looking as lovely as you do at your age, Allie. Are you thirty? If you are not, you must be perilously close."

"Piers!" she said, shocked.

"Very ungentlemanly of me to have noticed that you were past your eighteenth year, is it not?" he said. "But I am right, I will wager. Let me see. You were fifteen when Web confided to me his undying passion for you. He was three-and-twenty at the time, which would have made me two-and-twenty. Now let me see . . .'' He tapped one gloved finger against his chin and looked up at the sky. ''Yes, my dear Allie. That makes you very close to thirty if not right on it. But quite as lovely as you were at fifteen.'' He grinned and made her an elegant bow in the middle of the pavement on Oxford Street.

''Piers!'' she said again, laughing.

He extended one arm to her. ''Let me take you for tea and cakes,'' he said.

''Cakes?'' She looked up into his face and took his arm. ''I had luncheon little more than an hour ago.''

He looked down at her very trim waistline and pursed his lips. ''Definitely cakes,'' he said. ''The kind that ooze cream from both sides no matter how genteelly one bites into them. The kind one always has in one's hand when some dowager duchess comes along to be condescending. You really do look very fine, Allie. You are turning heads.''

''Oh, nonsense!'' she said. ''I am not even wearing my new bonnet.''

He settled her at a table in a confectioner's and ordered tea and cakes. He sat and smiled at her.

''You have escaped from your sister-in-law?'' he said. ''I take it the invalids are no longer at death's door.''

''They never were,'' she said. ''They had measles, not the pox, Piers. Phoebe has a free afternoon, Amanda being one of a party that is quite well chaperoned.''

''Poor Phoebe,'' he said. ''Her nose is out of joint over that, I would wager. It must be quite lowering to have nothing better to do with one's time than tend to ailing children.''

''You are being unkind,'' she said.

''Yes, I am,'' he agreed amiably, smiling at her and showing not one visible sign of contrition. ''I have just had the most amusing morning, Allie. I am excessively glad I ran into you, or I would have been forced to laugh aloud on Oxford Street and all to myself. Not at all a tonnish thing to do, at a guess.''

"I imagine you are right," she said, frowning over the plate of cakes that had been set down before them and selecting the one that looked least sinful. Then she looked indignantly at her companion, who was lounging back in his chair, his long legs stretched beneath the table. "You are not going to have one, are you?''

"No," he said. "I have to watch my waistline. Unlike you, Allie, there can be no doubt whatsoever of the fact that I have passed my thirtieth birthday.''

"Wretch!" she said, biting into pink icing.

"I had a letter yesterday," he said, "a timid and apologetic and self-effacing letter from a lady I had not seen in fifteen years.''

"Indeed?" she said. "I hope this is not going to turn into an improper story, Piers.''

"Oh, Lord, no," he said. "She was—and is—very respectable. Widow of a close acquaintance of mine at Cambridge—Margam. Lord Margam, I would have you know. The poor man hated being a baron. He would have liked nothing more than to spend his entire life lost in a dusty university library. Never had a penny to his name, even though there was a Lady Margam and an infant. I didn't know he was dead, poor chap. I haven't seen him for years.''

"His widow wrote to you?" she prompted.

"Yes." He chuckled. "It is all vastly amusing, Allie. The infant is now a hopeful young lady about to be loosed on society. Except that the mother doesn't know quite how to loose her, having spent the last dozen years or more rusticating somewhere. I am to be the entrance door, so it seems. The letter was larded with compliments, as you may imagine.''

"You are to introduce the girl into society?" Alice said.

"Be careful you don't choke on your cake," he said, looking at her assessingly. "I told you this was vastly amusing, did I not? And I have not got to the funny part yet." He looked down at the plate of cakes and up at her in some amusement. "You might as well have it, Allie. You have been wanting it since the plate was set down before you." He reached out, picked up a pastry that looked to be all air and cream, and set it down on her plate.

"Piers!" she said indignantly. "I have not glanced at it even once."

"Eat it anyway," he said. "It would be a shame to waste it. Lady Margam is staying with her brother on Russell Square. I called on them this morning. I have never been so diverted in my life."

He grinned at his memories and watched her take the first bite out of the pastry.

"He is a cit," he said, "and quite as vulgar as they come. He has about as much subtlety as a ten ton boulder. He wants me to marry the girl, of course."

"Did he say so?" Alice was caught with the pastry halfway to her mouth.

"Oh, dear, no," he said. "I am to discover all on my own that the girl is irresistible and adorable. He is a quite delightful character, Allie. I mean it. I would spend an hour in his company sooner than I would spend half as long with some of our more respectable lords. Never a dull moment."

"And are you going to do it?" Alice asked.

"Marry her?" he said. "Or precipitate her into society? Perhaps both. I have agreed to escort Miss Borden and her mama to the theater tomorrow evening. Bosley would not hear of coming himself, of course. He is afraid, I would guess, that he will fill the theater with the smell of fish."

"Fish?"

"He made his fortune in it," he said. "And a sizable one, too, from all accounts. It is my considered guess that he is paying the shot to have the girl fired off."

"And the girl herself, Piers?" she asked. "Miss Borden, did you say?"

He laughed. "A veritable innocent straight from the cradle," he said. "All lowered lashes and peeping eyes and blushing cheeks and ringlets. Quite adorable, I might add, if one likes the infantry."

"And do you?" she asked sharply.

He grinned. "Very appetizing," he said. "I shall have to see, Allie. I must confess that the uncle-in-law I would acquire is a definite attraction. And don't look indignant on his behalf. I am not making fun. I am serious."

"Piers," she said, dabbing the corners of her mouth with her napkin. "This is all a joke to you, is it not? This searching for a bride, I mean. It is not a joke. Your whole future happiness is at stake."

"And you think I could not be happy with a blushing infant?" he asked.

"Be serious, Piers," she said. "You know you could not. What would you talk about with the girl for the rest of your life?"

"I imagine I could make cooing noises to amuse her for most of the time," he said. "It could be vastly diverting, Allie."

"Oh," she said crossly, "Web should be here now. He would talk sense into you."

He took the napkin from her hand and rubbed her chin with it. "It is a good thing that dowager duchess is not here to observe you, Allie," he said. "You might have been mortified to discover afterward that there was cream on your chin. You blush almost as rosily as Miss Borden, you know. And how do you know that I cannot talk good sense to the infant? You have not met her."

"No, I have not," she agreed.

"Then you must do so," he said, "and pass judgment only afterward. Come to the theater with us tomorrow night. I think I may need you for moral support, anyway."

"You do not need three ladies," she said. "That would play altogether too much on your conceit."

"Now don't play hard to get, Allie," he said. "Seriously, I was planning to call on you later, even if I had to risk the danger of a house full of measles in order to do so, to ask you to accompany me. Should I invite another gentleman or two? I will if you think I ought.''

"Yes," she said. "I think that would be quite proper, Piers. But wait." She set her teacup down on its saucer and frowned into it for a moment. "I shall invite someone, if I may."

He raised his eyebrows. "Suitors, Allie?" he said. "And I have been feeling sorry for the fact that you have been shut up in a sickroom all the time since your arrival."

"He is not a suitor," she said. "And I did not meet him here. He is an acquaintance newly arrived from Bath. He called on me this morning and invited me to the theater one evening. This will work out well."

"I hope I am not expected to turn my back while the two of you bill and coo in the shadows of my box," he said. "I understand such behavior is not considered quite genteel. He followed you here, did he, Allie? And he is not a suitor? I shall have to see this man who cannot bear to see you absent from Bath for three days without following on your heels but is not your suitor. He had better not be a damned fortune hunter."

"Nonsense," she said. "Don't be foolish. He is as rich as Croesus."

"Then he is after your body," he said, getting to his feet and pulling back her chair for her. "And I can only applaud his taste. Still blushing, Allie? Tomorrow evening it is, then?"

"Tomorrow evening," she said. "I shall inspect your infant and give my opinion."

"And I shall inspect your Romeo," he said, "and give mine."

Alice stood up. "Romeo!" she said and laughed.

# 3

PHOEBE CARPENTER was not at all happy to hear that her sister-in-law was to attend the theater the following evening, even though Alive drove to Portman Square immediately after breakfast and remained until late afternoon. She read endlessly to Mary, whose eyesight was declared too much at risk from the infection to allow of her reading to herself. And she played spillikins with Richard and listened with cheerful interest to his enthusiastic accounts of his brother's various escapades at Oxford.

But Phoebe was very disgruntled and peevish.

"I do think you might have put your brother's family before your own pleasures for just a couple of weeks," she said.

"Mary and Richard are convalescing quite nicely," Alice said. "You need not have the smallest qualm about leaving them to their nurse's care for an evening, Phoebe. I shall return in the morning."

"Amanda has only an invitation to a concert, which she does not at all wish to attend," Phoebe said crossly. "We will remain at home. But still, Alice, you might have thought of the predicament you would have put us in if you had wanted to attend the theater tomorrow night. It is Lady Partiton's ball and like to be one of the biggest squeezes of the Season."

"I did not bring you all the way from Bath so that you might indulge in frivolity," Bruce chose to add at that moment.

Alice smiled at him. "Don't provoke yourself,

Bruce,'' she said. "I brought myself, if you will remember.''

"Well,'' her brother said, "you will be so independent, Alice. It is not at all the thing. Not when you have a brother to see to your needs.''

"The children will be as right as rain within the next few days,'' Alice said briskly. "I would recommend a short drive for them tomorrow if the good weather continues. Fresh air will do them the world of good.''

Phoebe shrieked and pressed a handkerchief to her lips.

Altogether, Alice thought as she was riding through the streets of London on her way home, she was not sorry that she had agreed to join Piers' theater party. It would be lovely to dress up for a formal occasion again and to watch a play. And she felt a great curiosity to see Miss Borden and her mama. As for herself, the chance to satisfy Sir Clayton Lansing by including him in the party was not to be missed. After this evening she would consider her duty done and would politely but firmly refuse any further invitations. It was to be hoped that he would take himself back home to Bath within a few days.

It seemed that Sir Clayton had other ideas. Alice engaged him in polite small talk in the carriage on the way to the theater and was somewhat disappointed to find that the box Piers had taken for the evening was still empty when they arrived. She hoped the rest of the party would not be long in coming.

"My dear Mrs. Penhallow," Sir Clayton said, seating her in the box with courtly care and bowing to her before taking his own seat beside her, "how you do outshine all the other ladies present.''

She smiled at him. "It is a very splendid theater, is it not?'' she said.

"I knew you would, of course," he said, "but now I am sure of it. I must be the envy of every other gentleman present.''

"How kind of you to say so," she murmured.

"Have you seen this play before, sir? I have been assured that it is well worth watching."

"I doubt I will be able to force my eyes to turn to the stage," he said, "when there is something far more delightful to look at—or should I say some*one*?"

"I do hope Mr. Westhaven and his party will not miss the beginning of the performance," she said.

"Do you have a long acquaintance with the gentleman, ma'am?" he asked. "And must I be jealous of him?"

"I have known him all my life," she said. "He was a particular friend of my late husband's. And mine, too."

"Ah," he said, smiling, "then I will not be jealous. For if you have known him all your life, ma'am, and he is still just a friend, I will suppose he can never be more to you or you to him."

This speech was delivered with a great deal of smiling and bowing. Alice was glad she had brought a fan with her. She used it, though the theater was not yet overly hot. And she gazed about her with a deliberate interest. If Piers was much longer, she would throttle him. If he failed altogether to put in an appearance, she would borrow a dueling pistol and shoot him.

And of course, she thought, Sir Clayton's final words ringing in her head, Piers would always be just a friend. Of course she would never mean more to him. She had known that from the time she had been fourteen, as thin and flat as a blade of grass, her hair still in long braids and herself almost totally invisible to the gentleman. She had feared it the following year when he and Web were coming home and she had finally persuaded her father to let her put her hair up and had looked with satisfaction at her newly developing figure in the glass. She had known it for sure as soon as they did come home and she saw the look of warm admiration in Webster Penhallow's eyes and the look of appreciative amusement in Piers'.

She had known it during the two and a half years of Web's courtship, while he waited for her to grow up and reach marriageable age. And on her wedding day when Piers had taken her waist between his hands and kissed her cheek and smiled with twinkling amusement at her blushing face and told her quite outrageously that he envied Web more than he could say for a wedding night to look forward to with an innocent and timid bride.

She had known it through nine years of marriage, when he had been more like a member of their family during the long spells when he was at home than just a very close and dear friend. He and Web had always been like brothers. His relationship with her during those nine years had been light and teasing and comfortable, though he had cried with her over Nicholas and she with him over Harriet and the stillborn daughter she had been too long giving birth to. And when he had posted down from London after Web's death, he had held her close for a full, silent hour, rocking her against him, soothing her numb pain, crying for both her and himself, though she herself had been unable to know the relief of tears.

Yes, Piers had always been a friend and always would be, she fervently hoped. For life would lose its final light if that friendship were ever withdrawn. And friendship was enough. She enjoyed her freedom and independence. She wanted no more than friendship from any man.

"You have a classically beautiful profile," Sir Clayton said. "I have been sitting silently here, admiring it, ma'am."

Alice smiled and began a new round of small talk. Would Piers never get there?

Miss Cassandra Borden was late going to her room to dress for the evening at the theater, though her mother fretted at the lengthy delay. Mr. Bosley had been giving the girl advice on how to fix her interest with Mr. Westhaven.

"You must always wear your costliest frocks and jewels, Cassie," he had said. "Tonight, of course, you will not have much choice of frock as most of your new rig-out has not been delivered yet. But you must wear the rubies, for sure. I am glad I had the foresight to buy them and the garnets and emeralds yesterday. Wear the necklace, the bracelet, and the earrings. Oh, and the brooch, too, of course. And finger them, Cassie, as if you did not know you did so. Then he will look at them and know how costly they are.''

''Yes, Uncle,'' she said.

''But a young girl cannot wear rubies, brother,'' Lady Margam said. ''It will be more proper for Cassandra to wear the pearls you sent her for her last birthday.''

''Mere baubles!'' he said dismissively.

''Come along, Cassandra,'' her mother said. ''It is time to get ready. It does not do to keep a gentleman waiting, you know.''

Mr. Bosley roared with laughter. ''There is nothing better,'' he said. ''Keep them hopping, Cassie. Keep them on their toes. Keep them anxious.''

''Yes, Uncle,'' she said.

''And smile at him, Cass,'' he said, ''and flutter your eyelashes in that way you girls have. And look at him as if you thought he was the only gentleman worth looking at. He will be at your feet in a week.''

''Will he, Uncle?'' she said.

''Come along, Cassandra,'' her mother said.

And finally they went.

The ladies were not yet ready, Mr. Westhaven was informed when he stepped punctually from his carriage and was admitted to the house on Russell Square. But it probably would not have mattered if they had been. It seemed that his host had decided to entertain and impress him.

Mr. Westhaven accepted a chair in a tastelessly but expensively decorated sitting room, took a glass of port from Mr. Bosley, and prepared to be entertained.

He was not disappointed. Interspersed with comments on horses and politics and boxing mills were details of just how large a fortune was to be made in fish and just how eager an enormously wealthy and single and lonely gentleman was to settle a large portion of his fortune on an only niece.

"When she see fit to marry, of course, sir," a genial Mr. Bosley said, beaming at his guest. "I would not consider it wise or good business to let my hard-earned pounds rest in the palm of a mere female. Cass's home would probably be full to overflowing with bonnets and feathers and fans."

Mr. Westhaven joined in the hearty laughter. No, that would not be wise at all, he assured his host. Better far to entrust the fortune to the girl's husband.

"When she sees fit to marry, of course," he added, and laughed with his host again.

He was vastly entertained. He could not remember when he had been more diverted. It was a pity he would have to wait until the next day to share his amusement with Allie. Doubtless he would not be able to have a single private word with her that evening, what with his responsibility to entertain Miss Borden and her mama and Allie's preoccupation with this fellow from Bath, who had better not turn out to be a fortune hunter after all, if he knew what was good for him.

His amusement was complete when a servant opened the door to admit the two ladies. He rose to his feet and bowed. Lady Margam looked all that was proper for the occasion. And so did Miss Borden, by Jove! Piers thought. She looked quite exquisitely pretty in white satin and lace, her hair in masses of auburn ringlets, her eyes lowered, her cheeks becomingly flushed. She wore a single strand of pearls at her throat, doubtless the mother's influence. He had half expected to find her loaded to the ground with costly and vulgar jewels of the fond uncle's choosing.

But it was as much amusement as admiration he felt as he helped the girl on with her wrap and ushered both ladies out to his waiting carriage. Amusement that he found himself in such a situation, about to ap-

pear before the *ton* with a blushing member of the
infantry, and singled out quite markedly by her uncle
as an eligible husband. Mr. Bosley must be well aware
of the baron's title that was so close to being his, he
thought. Perhaps he was not as well aware of the fact
that the present baron was in his early sixties and hale
and hearty enough to live to be a hundred. And perhaps he did not know that Mr. Westhaven need not fall
all over himself for that fishy fortune, being a very
wealthy man in his own right.

Good Lord, he thought, taking his seat in the carriage opposite the two ladies, he did not even know
what color the girl's eyes were. He pursed his lips and
concentrated on not laughing aloud. He began to talk,
using only the surface of his mind to do so. He had a
feeling that what he had said to Allie about cooing to
the girl most of the time was probably not a gross
exaggeration. The mother was reasonably sensible; the
girl was mute.

Thank goodness Allie was at the theater before him,
he thought fifteen minutes later. Of course, it would
be strange if she were not, since there were barely five
minutes left before the start of the performance. He
grinned at her behind the backs of his ladies and exchanged bows with her escort. The introductions were
made.

Sir Clayton Lansing was a handsome enough man,
he supposed after a brief penetrating glance before he
seated first Lady Margam and then Miss Borden. He
took his own seat next to the latter and asked her if
she was in any draft from the door. He did so merely
for the amusement and pleasure of seeing her eyes peep
up at him from beneath those lowered lashes and of
hearing her whispered, "No, I thank you, sir. You are
very kind."

Lansing was well enough for those females who
liked long, thin males with long, thin faces and hair
that had been plastered to the head for neatness after
being parted with ruthless symmetry down one side.
Perhaps it was Allie he should have been asking about

drafts. But not from doorways. The man was leaning close enough to be sending drafts down her gown to her toes.

She looked remarkably handsome in a dark green gown with Web's diamonds at her throat. But then Allie always did look handsome, he thought. No matter what time of day he had walked in on her and Web—and he had walked in at all hours—she had always been neat and elegant.

It was strange to see her with another man. A man who was not Web, that was. They had been a devoted couple. Theirs had been everyone's dream of the perfect marriage. For the last several years before his friend's death he had ceased to think of them as separate individuals. They had been Web-and-Allie, his dearest friends.

Strange, really, when he and Web had been almost inseparable as boys and as young men. She had been Alice Carpenter, the rector's daughter, an awkward child during one visit home, an alluring young woman the next. She might have come between them, Web and him. But she had not. It had been so very obvious from the start that she loved his friend. She had made his short life a very happy one indeed. Piers had been quite unable to resent her—or Web.

It was strange to see her now with someone else. Strange to think of her with anyone else. She belonged to Web. He felt a quite unreasonable instinct to stride across the box, pick up the baronet and his chair both together, and set them down three feet farther from Allie than they now were.

The thought amused him so much that he had to purse his lips again. And he caught Alice's eye across the box and winked. She smiled back.

If he had expected to have to entertain his young guest with coos during the interval, Mr. Westhaven was agreeably surprised. Three young gentleman with whom he remembered to have only the most passing acquaintance had decided that they were his boon companions and called upon him in his box. It was very civil and sporting of them, as he remarked to Alice before the play resumed, when he had the chance to exchange a few words with her. He could not imagine what he had done to earn such cordial treatment.

All three young men exhibited identical surprise that their friend, Mr. Westhaven, was escorting a pretty young lady. They had not noticed her from the pit when they spotted their friend and decided to pay him their respects. But they all swallowed their disappointment at not being allowed ten minutes of the pleasure of his conversation, and set themselves to charming the little beauty.

"Their kindness is overwhelming," Mr. Westhaven said to Alice. And bending closer to whisper in her ear, he added, "Do you think they have heard of the fishy fortune?"

"Piers!" she said, and hid her explosion of laughter in a cough.

"All three of them are notoriously light in the pocket," he said.

There was time to say no more. His three newly acquired friends were taking their leave and Miss Borden was feeling faint.

"I shall take you outside into the corridor, my love," her mother was saying.

"Allow me, ma'am," Mr. Westhaven said, extending his arm to the girl. "Do lean on me, Miss Borden. I shall promenade you outside in the corridor and you will be feeling more the thing in a moment."

"Thank you," she said, looking up at him for a fleeting moment to reveal to his interested gaze a pair of fine green eyes. "I am being so foolish."

"Not at all," he said. "The theater is almost stuffy enough to give me the vapors, too. Indeed, if you had not needed my supporting arm just when you did, I believe I would have needed yours."

"Oh," she said, favoring him with an uncomprehending look from those eyes. Whoever had selected her gown, Mr. Westhaven thought with decided interest, had done so with the full knowledge that she had the bosom to do it justice.

"This is your first visit to a London theater, Miss Borden?" he asked conversationally. "And how are you enjoying it?"

"Oh, it is quite splendid!" she said breathlessly. "I thank you, sir. I just wish . . ."

He bent his head closer to hers. Her dark lashes had a most interesting way of fanning across her cheeks. And those cheeks were flushed again. She was one of those fortunate females whose necks did not become blotchy when they blushed.

"What is it you wish?" he asked.

"I just wish Mama and Uncle would not . . ." she said in a voice so small that he had to lower his head even closer to hers. "But I am sorry. Please forgive me."

"You are forgiven," he said promptly. "But what, pray, was the fault? What do you wish your mother and your uncle would not?"

She looked full into his eyes for a moment, her own large and troubled and trusting. Then she lowered them again.

"Try to marry me to you," she said.

Mr. Westhaven resisted the urge to shout with laughter. It would not, no, it certainly would not do, he thought. The child was a troubled infant. "And is that what they are trying to do?" he asked.

"Because you are to be Lord Berringer one day," she said in a breathless rush, "and because you are fashionable. And it is said you are in search of a wife."

"I see," he said. "But of course, your uncle and your mama will be eager to see to it that you make a suitable match now that you are of marriageable age. And so very lovely, too. I daresay they have not fixed their choice irrevocably on me. Soon you will be going to balls and routs and whatnot, and the young bucks will be killing each other for the favor of one of your smiles."

But there was no drawing a smile from her.

"Uncle says it must be you," she said.

"Does he?" Mr. Westhaven said, pursing his lips. "And you have no wish to marry someone in doddering old age? It is quite understandable, ma'am. I shall solve the problem by not offering for you, shall I?"

"It is not that," she said. "But I did not think it fair to you, sir. You would certainly not wish to be associated with my family, Uncle being not quite respectable, though I love him dearly, of course. He has always shown nothing but kindness to me."

Mr. Westhaven raised his eyebrows. "I have yet to be persuaded that being in trade makes a man less than respectable," he said.

"I am sorry," she said. "I wish I had not spoken. Indeed, I do."

"I do not," he said. "Shall we be friends, Miss Borden? And later, much, much later, we will both decide whether or not we wish to be something else? Come, that would be a comfortable arrangement, don't you agree?" He smiled at her, forcing amusement back and kindness to the fore. The poor infant. She must have been frightened out of her wits by two overbearing adults who between them were trying to take away all her freedom of choice.

"I would like that," she said, peeping up at him once more. "You are kind, sir."

"Not at all," he said, patting her hand in an avuncular manner and feeling the full amusement of his unaccustomed role. "Shall we return to my box? I believe the play is resuming."

A sweet and thoroughly delightful little infant, he thought a couple of minutes later as he turned his eyes toward the stage, his lips pursed. He could have shared his merriment, but his attention was soon caught by the action on stage. He did not feel Alice's eyes on him.

Alice felt justly punished for upsetting Phoebe and her brother by insisting on keeping her theater engagement rather than sitting with Mary and Richard. She had not had a pleasant evening.

She dismissed her maid later that night and climbed gratefully into bed. For the rest of her time in London—perhaps she would be able to get away in another week or so—she would content herself with the tedium of a sickroom that had no business being a sickroom any longer. Richard in particular should have been outdoors and using up some of his pent-up energy.

She had had some agreeable conversation with Lady Margam, who remembered Web, though he had not been such a particular friend of Lord Margam's as Piers had been. But on the whole the evening had been thoroughly disagreeable. There had been all the expenditure of energy on turning aside Sir Clayton's compliments and keeping the conversation light and inane. And there had been all the annoyance of seeing Piers dancing attendance on a shallow little girl, and knowing that there was every likelihood that he would end up marrying her or someone just like her.

Harriet had been just like her. Alice and Web had been horrified when he had returned to Westhaven Park after one of his absences, bringing with him a bride. Harriet had been very pretty and very sweet and very, very empty-headed. It had been painful to try to keep a conversation going with her.

Piers had treated her with amused indulgence. But it had been obvious to both of them that he did not find any companionship with his wife.

There had never been the smallest evidence that he mistreated Harriet, and no sign whatsoever that she was unhappy with him. Indeed, there was no indication that Piers himself was unhappy. Except that they knew him. Web had always known him, and she had known him for several years before he married. They had both known him well enough to detect signs of restlessness that would have been imperceptible to anyone else, Harriet included.

He had been distraught, suicidal even, on her death.

But had love been the cause? Or had it been something else?

"He does not have a cruel bone in his body, Allie, despite some of the outrageous things he says," Web had told her the night of the funeral, when Piers had finally staggered home, refusing their offer of hospitality for the night. "He did not love her, but that now is the trouble. He will blame himself for her death, you will see, because he did not love her and should not therefore have put her life at risk. We will have to keep a careful eye on him, love, mark my words."

And he had been quite right, of course.

Had Piers not learned from that experience that foolish young girls were not the right kind of bride for him?

Apparently not. Alice wished fiercely that Web were still alive. Not that he had been able to stop Piers that first time, of course. But then they had not known of the marriage until Piers had brought Harriet home.

It had been a worrying evening. And it had been capped by Sir Clayton's proposing to her in the carriage and even trying to kiss her. She had been forced to engage in a most undignified wrestling match, and had escaped the kiss only with the aid of some sharp words. It was a blessing indeed that she had not been forced to slap him. That would have been too mortifying for words.

She had refused his offer. But she feared that her natural reluctance to hurt another had made her refusal less than convincing. Certainly Sir Clayton had assured himself that he would do himself the honor of asking her again when she had had time to consider the advantages of such a match and would be taken less by surprise.

"For I realize, Mrs. Penhallow," he had said, "that you could have had no forewarning of the extent of my feelings."

Sometimes, Alice thought, sitting up in bed and punching her pillows, she longed for the dullness and peace of her life in Bath.

# 4

BRUCE was in a bad temper when Alice arrived at Portman Square soon after breakfast the following morning. Not that he was ever exactly sunny-natured, she thought with an inward sigh. But this morning he was more than ordinarily irritable. He had learned that his efforts to have his son reinstated at Oxford had been in vain. Jarvis would have to wait until the following year to resume his studies.

In addition to that annoyance, Phoebe was indisposed, and Bruce blamed Alice.

"For she has a great deal on her mind," he said, "what with the children sick, Jarvis in disgrace, and Amanda making her come-out. The least you could do, Alice, is have some family feeling and take some of the load from her shoulders."

"Which is exactly what I will do today," Alice said briskly. "I shall do what I can to entertain Richard and Mary this morning, and this afternoon, if the weather continues fine, I shall take them for a short drive."

"And give them both a chill?" he said. "I would have thought you had learned your lesson with Webster, Alice."

Alice bit her lip and decided not to retaliate. She retired to the nursery to a long and tedious day. The afternoon brought a little interest when Richard agreed to the drive—indeed, he would have liked nothing better than to take a horse and gallop in Hyde Park, but Alice laughingly suggested that he wait a few days for that pleasure.

"I can guarantee," she said, "that your legs will feel like jelly when you step out of doors, Richard. Being confined to a bed and a nursery for more than a week does that to a person, you know."

Mary refused to move from her bed, claiming that she had discovered more spots just that morning and was sickening for a second dose of the measles.

Alice joined Phoebe in the drawing room for tea. When she saw her sister-in-law, she felt guilty for all the uncharitable thoughts she had been entertaining all day. Phoebe was flushed and heavy-eyed, and her voice had a deeper tone than usual.

"I am hagged," was all she said when Alice asked after her health.

"You look feverish, Phoebe," Alice said. "Are you sure you should not be in bed?"

"I cannot take to my bed," Phoebe said, dabbing a handkerchief at her temples. "There is the Partiton ball this evening. Amanda cannot miss that of all things. It is to be the grandest occasion of the Season so far."

"But with so many entertainments every day," Alice said, seating herself behind the teapot since Phoebe made no move to do so, and proceeding to pour, "surely it will be no disaster to miss one. Amanda will understand, I am sure."

"It is out of the question," Phoebe said, laying her head back against a cushion and closing her eyes.

"Do you have a headache?" Alice asked.

"It will go away once I have drunk some tea," her sister-in-law replied.

"And a sore throat, Phoebe?"

Her sister-in-law did not reply.

Alice frowned and poured a cup of tea for herself. "Have you ever had the measles?" she asked.

Phoebe opened weary eyes. "I must have," she said. "All children have the measles, do they not? And Amanda and Jarvis had them as children."

"I remember," Alice said. "You wrote to tell me. Were you and Bruce not forced to leave your aunt's in

Kent sooner than you planned in order to return home to the children?''

"Ah, yes," Phoebe said vaguely.

"They were probably not infectious by the time you got home," Alice said. She set the teapot down. "I hope I am wrong, Phoebe, but I do believe you have taken the infection."

"Nonsense!" her sister-in-law said crossly. "Ladies of forty do not have the measles, Alice."

But measles or not, she was forced to agree to lie down immediately after tea, in the hope that she would feel well enough to attend the Partiton ball. By dinnertime, however, it was clear that she was not even well enough to come downstairs.

Bruce was in the blackest of moods, especially when Amanda, who had returned from a friend's house only an hour before, suggested that he accompany her to the ball instead of her mother.

"Out of the question," he said. "I am expected at Brooks'. If your mother is too ill, your aunt will have to take you instead.'

"Aunt Alice?" Amanda turned wide, anxious eyes on her. "Will you? Oh, please."

Alice felt a wave of amusement as she was being driven home a half hour later in Bruce's carriage in order that she might be ready in time to accompany Amanda to the ball. So much for her decision of the night before not to attend any other social event during her stay in London. She was about to appear at a grander ball than any she had every attended with Web during their infrequent visits to town. Even when she was to be merely a chaperon, it was a heady prospect. She doubted that she had any gown quite grand enough.

This business of choosing another bride was much like a game, Mr. Westhaven thought as he stood in the Partiton ballroom, quizzing glass in hand, surveying the crowd around him. A most diverting game, though one requiring considerable skill. For if one did not take care, one was likely to find oneself leg-shackled before one had quite steeled one's mind to relinquish one's freedom.

He could permit himself to look, even with the aid of his quizzing glass. He could permit himself to smile, to converse, to dance, to promenade with a sweet young thing on his arm. He could permit himself to charm the mamas. But he must always do all of those things in the plural. Always he must avoid singling out one particular beauty for more attention than all the rest.

He had led Lady Charlotte Maddingly into the opening set at the last ball, Miss Amanda Carpenter the one before that. He had taken Miss Brede driving in the park two days before and the Honorable Miss Willow two days before that. He had accompanied Miss Pomfret to the opera last week, the Honorable Miss Cassandra Borden to the theater the night before.

All of them were quite delightful. All of them were possible brides. All of them would have jumped at the chance to be the future Lady Berringer, he believed. Or if they did not, their mamas would certainly have jumped at it for them. But all must be done in perfect balance.

He was enjoying himself. It was vastly amusing to find that at the age of six-and-thirty he had still but to raise an eyebrow or a finger or a quizzing glass to raise hopes and blushes. And to know that such thoughts were not vanity at all. For whereas Mr. Piers Westhaven of Westhaven Park had never found himself lacking feminine company when he had needed it, Mr. Piers Westhaven, heir to Lord Berringer of Bingamen Hall, did not find himself lacking female company whether he needed it or not.

He was going to have to be careful, though. Very careful. For the balance of his attentions to sweet young creatures was about to be tipped. He had escorted Miss Borden to the theater last evening, and he was to lead her into the opening set tonight, always provided that she and her mama arrived in time, of course. The gossips would not be slow to note that particular mark of favor shown to the girl.

Bosley had invited him in for brandy the night before after he had returned the ladies safely to the house. Mr. Westhaven had been unable to deny himself the pleasure of another hour of the man's conversation.

He had not been disappointed. He had been entertained by a lengthy and fascinating account of the importance of bribes and a little blackmail to the businessman who wished to make more than a very modest fortune. Considering the probable wealth of his host, Mr. Westhaven had guessed that the man must have half the population of London within his power. A fascinating man, indeed.

How Bosley succeeded in interspersing with this topic the fact that he had wangled an invitation for his niece to the Partiton ball the next evening, Mr. Westhaven did not know. Though when he thought about it again, he guessed that there was some very real connection. No one except her mother was needed to take the girl to the ball, of course, but it would be a shame for such a pretty and such a very shy young lady to be without a partner at the start of the ball so that everyone might see how pretty she was and how daintily she danced.

"I don't know how these things are arranged, sir," Mr. Bosley said, "but my sister does not know anyone to introduce little Cassie to, you know."

Mr. Westhaven pursed his lips and pulled at his earlobe. It was too soon yet to make the obvious reply. It was too amusing to witness how his host would proceed.

"You may be sure that the hostess will see to it that there are no wallflowers," he said. "It would reflect on her skills."

"Ah," Mr. Bosley said. "You have set my mind at rest, sir. But Cass will hide in corners, the timid puss. What if the hostess does not notice her for half an evening?"

Mr. Westhaven raised his eyebrows. "Will your sister not ensure that that does not happen?" he asked.

Mr. Bosley sighed. "Right you are, sir," he said. "I am just too fond an uncle, you see, and too anxious to see my girl properly married and my fortune settled on a worthy gentleman before my passing."

"Your passing?" Mr. Westhaven asked, amazed. "Surely you are not ailing, sir? You look to be in the very best of health."

Mr. Bosley had laughed heartily and changed the subject. And only then had Mr. Westhaven suggested, as if the idea had not been pressed upon him at all, that he would be honored to lead Miss Borden into the opening set at the Partiton ball.

At least, he thought now, continuing to gaze about him and nodding genially to a pair of smiling dowagers, he had felt as if he had not been pressed into it. He would have to watch Bosley. And himself. He must not single out Miss Borden for any more attentions within the week.

Unless he decided that all his attentions for the rest of his life must center on her, of course. She was a deliciously pretty little infant. Though, of course, she had suggested quite strongly to him the evening before that she did not wish to be pressed into a marriage with him.

Besides, he thought, spotting Miss Carpenter across the room with Alice, the idea of making love to the girl, of actually bedding her, seemed almost obscene. She was just a child. A luscious child

And what on earth was Allie doing here, he thought, without the merest hint to him the night before that such was her plan? He made his way across the room to her and noted her appearance as he did so. A simple high-waisted gown of deep blue satin, completely unadorned, its neckline low but not indiscreetly so, Web's unostentatious diamonds at her throat, her dark hair smooth and shining, with only a few curls at the neck, no turban or feathers.

She was by far the most plainly dressed woman

present. She made them all look like so many gaudy and fussy bandboxes.

"Good evening, Miss Carpenter," he said, bowing to the girl. He took Alice's hand in his and raised it to his lips. "What on earth are you doing here, Allie? Apart from outshining everyone else, that is."

"What nonsense you speak," she said, laughing. "Is this your courtly behavior, Piers, paying outrageous compliments and kissing hands? I am here chaperoning Amanda. Phoebe, I fear, is coming down with the measles."

"How mortifying at her, ah, age," he said. "So you are to find a place in a dusty corner with all the other faded creatures, are you, Allie, watching with sharp eyes to make sure that no young buck—or old one, for that matter—clasps your niece's waist with too much enthusiasm or takes her beyond the terrace when the need for fresh air is upon her?"

"Something like that," she said, glancing at Amanda, who was conversing with a group of young acquaintances. "I do regret the fact that I left my lorgnette at home, though. I fear I will not look nearly stern enough without it."

He grinned at her. "The second set is a waltz," he said. "You must dance it with me, Allie."

"Absolutely not," she said, horrified. "I have not come to dance, Piers. And the waltz! Never."

His eyes danced with amusement. "Do you consider it very improper?" he asked. "Will you swoon quite away even to watch others dance it? It is quite fashionable and considered quite proper, I do assure you. And I know you know the steps. I have not forgotten you and Web dancing it in your drawing room."

"That was only so that we might all laugh and agree how ridiculous it was," she said indignantly. "You know it was, Piers."

"Anyway," he said, "you must dance it with me, Allie. Very few of the infantry are allowed to do it. They have to be approved first by society's dragons. If you will not dance with me, I must be a wallflower, and I should never live down the ignominy.''

''How ridiculous!'' she said, laughing despite herself. ''Better to be a wallflower than a public spectacle, Piers. I should trip all over your feet.''

''Never in a thousand nights, ma'am,'' he said. ''Do you think I do not know how to lead? Come, Allie, your answer. I see that lady Margam and Miss Borden are here, and I must dance attendance on them. I am to lead Miss Borden into the opening set. She looks quite delectable, doesn't she? More ringlets than last night, would you say? Is it possible?''

''She looks very pretty, Piers,'' she said. ''The orchestra is about to begin, and Lord and Lady Partiton have come from the receiving line. You must go.''

He took her wrist between a thumb and forefinger and winked at her. ''Not until you have agreed to that waltz,'' he said. ''I shall remain chained to you like this for the rest of the evening if you do not.''

''Piers!'' she said, laughing. ''This is blackmail. Oh, very well, then. Go!''

He strolled over to Miss Cassandra Borden, who was standing beside her mama, her eyes directed at the floor. Yes, quite deliciously lovely in an apricot-colored confection. He smiled and bowed at the mother and set himself to putting the girl at her ease.

Alice had certainly not intended to dance. For one thing, she was not dressed fittingly. She was very conscious of the plainness of her dress in comparison with all the finery she saw about her. For another, she had had no experience with grand balls. She had attended dances in the country with Web, but there was very little comparison between those affairs and the grandeur of this. And finally, she had come in the role of chaperon. She was Amanda's widowed aunt.

Besides, she did not know anyone at the ball except Piers and Amanda. And Lady Margam, of course, and Cassandra. And Jarvis appeared before the first set ended, with a group of young companions, all hiding their youth in a dandified appearance.

"I say," Jarvis said when he came across the room to greet her, "who is the beauty dancing with Mr. Westhaven? Can you secure me an introduction, Aunt Alice?"

Piers himself made the introductions when the set came to an end, and Jarvis was fortunate enough to engage Cassandra for the set of country dances that was to follow the waltz. It looked as if the girl would not lack for partners.

In the meantime, Lady Partiton had presented Lord Maisey to Alice, and she had agreed to dance the same set of country dances with him. And then Sir Clayton put in an appearance and engaged her for a quadrille later in the evening.

"You must reserve the waltz after supper for me, Allie," Piers said as he led her away from Sir Clayton's effusive compliments. "Otherwise your card will fill up and I will have no one sensible to talk to for the rest of the evening. Do you have a card, by the way?"

"Of course not," she said. "I am a chaperone."

"Ah, yes," he said. "I hate to tell you this, Allie, but you forgot your lace cap, you know. A chaperon looks quite undressed without it. Not that I wish to discompose you, of course."

She smiled.

"You are also forgetting to trip over my toes," he said a minute later. "Indeed, Allie, I believe you have been spending these months taking secret dancing lessons in Bath. Have you? Is Lansing your dancing master, by any chance? He certainly minces about as if he might be."

"You are being unkind and absurd," she said. "You told me yourself that you lead well in the dance. You do."

"Ah," he said, and grinned down at her until she felt like giggling like a girl.

For it was, she was discovering, quite the most exhilarating feeling in the world to dance in such a large ballroom to music provided by a whole orchestra, instead of just a pianoforte and fiddle. And with Piers. She had never suspected that he was an accomplished dancer, though he had, of course, taught her and Web the steps of the waltz during that rainy afternoon when they had all laughed so much and agreed that it was quite the silliest dance ever to have been invented.

It was not. On the contrary, it was quite the most wonderful dance in the whole world.

"You are not supposed to be smiling and glowing with such enjoyment, Allie," her partner said, amused.

"Why not?" she asked, sobering immediately.

"It is unfashionable," he said. "Just look about you. You see the striped-waistcoated gentleman with the shirt points in imminent danger of piercing his eyeballs?"

She nodded.

"The Duke of Eccles' offspring," he said. "And all the gentlemen with him? All of the very highest *ton*, my dear. And the ladies over there?" He nodded in the direction of the west wall. "Not one of them without some sort of title. What do they all have in common?"

"Oh, nothing at all as far as I can see," she said. "You must solve the riddle for me, Piers."

"All bored out of their pea brains," he said. "They are all competing to see who can look most as if he wished he were somewhere—anywhere in the world—rather than right here. They are in fashion, Allie. That is the fashionable look for this Season. To be imitated at all costs if you wish to appear to be one of them. Now, enough of these smiles. Give me a look of boredom."

"Piers," she said, her smile spreading again until it threatened to burst out into laughter, "you are quite the most absurd person I have ever known."

"Whatever you do," he said, looking at her in some horror, "don't let loose with that laughter, Allie. I would be mortified beyond words. I doubt I would have the nerve to show my face at any other entertainment for the rest of the Season.''

"Seriously," she said, "they do look bored, don't they? Oh, I wonder why. They must have everything in the world to make them happy."

"Except something with which to stimulate their brains," he said. "But I tell you, Allie, it really is not the thing to appear to enjoy yourself. I tell you only the sober truth. You do not think I would lie to you, do you?"

She smiled as he grinned at her again. And she became aware, as she had when he had been dancing with Cassandra Borden earlier, that eyes followed him about the floor. Just because he was the new heir to Lord Berringer? she wondered. But that was absurd. The room was full of gentlemen who already had titles, not just the expectation of them. Although Lord Berringer was reputed to be one of the wealthiest of the nobility, he was by no means one of the most exalted.

No, Alice thought, the foolish man quite misinterpreted the interest the *ton* was showing in him. For most of his life he had scorned tonnish events, avoiding balls and such during his stays in London. Now he was attending those events and dressing accordingly. And he was in search of a wife.

The combination was irresistible. For Piers, quite unknown to himself, it seemed, was easily the most handsome and attractive man in the ballroom. And it was not just her partial eyes that saw him thus. The eyes of many other female guests told the same story.

"So which one should I marry, Allie?" he asked, his customary look of ironic amusement replacing the grin. "There is a wide choice, is there not? Can you advise me?"

"Gracious, no," she said. "I am no matchmaker, Piers."

"Maybe I should move to the East and set up a harem," he said.

"You would probably find it as difficult to narrow

the choice to one hundred and fifty as you do now to one," she said.

He laughed and spun her into a turn at the corner of the ballroom.

"Will you allow me to escort you and your niece home at the end of the evening?" he asked. "I shall probably spend the rest of the night at one of my clubs otherwise, Allie, and will wake up about noon tomorrow with a thick head. Dreadful habits one acquires in town."

"Why do you not spend some time at Westhaven Park, then?" she asked.

He looked down at her. "I told you why," he said. "It is lonely there, Allie, without either you or Web. If you had not taken yourself off to Bath, I doubtless would go home more often."

"Well," she said.

"Will you let me escort you home?"

Alice thought of Sir Clayton Lansing, with whom she had promised to dance later in the evening.

"That would be pleasant," she said.

Mr. Westhaven had sent the Carpenter carriage home, to the joy of the coachman and footman, who had an unexpectedly early night for a change. He conveyed the ladies home in his own carriage, escorting Amanda to the door of the house on Portman Square and then vaulting back into his carriage to take Alice to Cavendish Square.

"Will you invite me in, Allie?" he asked when they got there. "For tea or coffee or water or something? I feel like talking to someone sensible."

"At this hour?" she said. "Do you have any idea what time it is, Piers?"

"Just for a short while?" he asked. "Come on, Allie."

"And do you realize how very improper it would be for me to entertain you alone at this hour?" she asked. "No, you do not, do you?"

"What nonsense," he said. "We are such very old friends, after all."

"You can keep your 'old's' to yourself, thank you," she said. "Oh, come along, then. I shall not sleep for guilt if I turn you away."

"Good girl," he said. "Will your man insist on standing at my shoulder, glowering?"

"Perkins?" she said. "Not at all. He will be sent to bed, as he always is as soon as I come home. You will have to come to my sitting room, Piers, since the lamps have all been extinguished in the other rooms. And it will have to be chocolate, I'm afraid. That is what I always have at bedtime."

"Chocolate sounds quite appetizing," he said, handing her from the carriage and instructing his coachman to go home. He would walk, he explained. "You are not annoyed with me, are you, Allie?"

She clucked her tongue. "Why should I be annoyed?" she said. "What could possibly annoy me about being coerced into entertaining a gentleman in my sitting room after midnight?"

"Quite so," he said, grinning down at her as her manservant slid the bolts back and opened the door.

# 5

MR. WESTHAVEN sank into a chair and looked about him.

"This is cozy, Allie," he said. "You must have a gift for creating coziness. It was always there at Chandlos. I used to think it was the design and size of the house that made it so much more comfortable than Westhaven, but I see now it was your touch." He yawned as Alice handed him a cup of chocolate.

She picked up her embroidery and seated herself on a love seat. She bent her head to her work.

He watched her for a while. "You aren't going to marry that Lansing, are you?" he asked.

She looked up startled. "Gracious," she said, "of course not. I am not planning to marry anyone."

"Good," he said. "He is too thin."

"What an absurd reason for objecting to my marrying him," she said with a smile. "I take it you *are* objecting?"

"And his smile is too oily," he said.

"Poor Sir Clayton," she said. "He tries his very best to be agreeable, and someone objects to his smile."

"And his hair matches the smile," he said.

Alice laughed despite herself. "But it is always neat, Piers," she said. "You must grant him that."

"Has he asked you?" he asked. "I'll wager he has."

"Last night," she said, "when we were returning from the theater. I refused him, of course. But it was kind of him to offer."

"Kind!" he said, picking up his cup and sipping the hot liquid. "Allie, have you looked at yourself in the mirror lately? Don't let him harass you. He obviously has not been discouraged, judging by the way he was hovering over you tonight at every chance. I'll plant him a facer if he keeps on bothering you."

Alice gave a gurgle of laughter. "What a delightful *on dit* for the *ton* that would be," she said. "Do make sure you are in the middle of someone's ballroom when you do it, Piers."

He chuckled and lounged back in his chair, watching her stitch her embroidery. He yawned again.

"What do you think of Miss Borden?" he asked.

"She is very pretty," she said, "and very alluring, I believe, despite her shyness. Certainly she attracted a great deal of attention this evening. I do not believe she missed a single set, except for the waltzes, of course."

"Do you think I should marry her?" he asked.

"Piers." She looked at him imploringly. "No!"

"Because I am too old for her?" he asked. "I am not quite decrepit, Allie. I am still capable of a number of activities associated with youth." He grinned at her bowed head. "I love making you blush."

"Your age has nothing to do with it," she said. "If you loved the girl and she loved you, I would urge you to the marriage. But then, if that were so, you would not be asking my opinion at all."

"Perhaps I could love her, too," he said. "She is pretty enough, as you say, Allie. And she has other charms. And she is very biddable."

"Oh, Piers," she said, resting her right hand on her work and looking up at him. "Does love mean no more to you than that?"

"Well," he said, smiling wickedly at her, "if I am to spend the rest of my life looking at a woman and lying next to her at night, her appearance is of some significance."

"But that is not love," she said, exasperated. She picked up her needle again and stitched on.

"What is, then?" he said. "Tell me, Allie."

"It is physical attraction, of course," she said. "But there is so very much more than that, Piers. If it were only beauty, what would happen when the couple grew old? There has to be a mutual respect and liking, a mutuality of mind, a companionship, a friendship."

"And that is it? That is all?" he asked, smiling at the top of her head.

"And something else," she said quietly. "Something in addition to all those things. Something that words cannot express. A certain magic." She spoke more firmly. "And above all, there has to be a determination from the start to make the other happy, to put the other's comfort and joy before one's own."

"Allie," he said fondly, "all the world would be bachelor or spinster if your definition held. I might be looking forever and never find a bride. I might never breed those heirs of mine."

She said nothing, but stitched on. He finished drinking his chocolate and put his head back against the cushions of the chair. He closed his eyes.

"What I should do," he said, "is marry you, Allie. Don't you think that would be a good idea?"

"Gracious!" she said, her hand stranded in midair. "No, Piers!"

But he was grinning at her, his head turned sideways on the cushion. "Have I outraged you?" he said. "I'm sorry, Allie. I was just teasing. I wouldn't insult you by making you an offer."

"Insult me?" She frowned.

"I would be a poor bargain, wouldn't I?" he said. "A fellow like me. After Web. Do you find living without him very hard, Allie?"

She threaded her needle through her work and folded it neatly and deliberately. "No," she said. "I cannot dwell on the past, Piers. It would be to deny the wonder of life. I was fortunate to have him for nine years. I have no regrets about those years. I did my best to make him contented, and he devoted his life to my happiness. Even Nicholas I would not erase from my life, despite all the pain of losing him. But all the grieving and pining and moping in the world will not bring either of them back. I have to live on. I have to find happiness with what is left. And I am well blessed. I do not find living difficult.''

The smile remained only in his eyes. ''You and Web had the love you described, didn't you?'' he said.

She drew circles on her palm. After a while she nodded.

''And that leaves me,'' he said. ''I am taking Miss Borden driving tomorrow afternoon, you know. Or I suppose I mean this afternoon. Do you think that after last night at the theater, tonight at the ball, and tomorrow afternoon in the park, old Bosley will be having the banns read?''

''I do not know Mr. Bosley,'' she said, smiling at him. ''But I think perhaps he will wait for a more formal offer. Do have a care, though, Piers, unless you have definitely decided that Miss Borden is the girl you wish to make your bride.''

''I really did not intend to single her out for more attention within the next week,'' he said. ''But she told me over supper that all the other young bucks who surrounded her this evening frightened her. She was afraid that they were going to be calling on her uncle and inviting her out. She seemed truly terrified at the prospect and looked very grateful when I suggested forestalling them by calling early on her uncle myself and offering to take her driving. She actually looked full at me for a whole second. I think she must see me as a father figure, don't you, Allie?''

She laughed. ''A father figure? You?'' she said. ''I shall say to you what you said to me awhile ago, Piers. Have you looked at yourself in the mirror lately?''

''That bad, eh?'' he said ruefully. ''Do you think your servants are tossing and turning in their beds, afraid for your virtue, Allie?''

''I would not be at all surprised,'' she said. ''This is highly improper, you know.''

''But you don't really mind, do you?'' he asked,

getting to his feet. "It's just me. You know you are perfectly safe with me, don't you, Allie?"

"Yes," she said, smiling. "But it is quite scandalously late. After two o'clock. Good night, Piers."

"Good night, Allie," he said, setting his hands at her waist. "Thank you for letting me come in. You have made me feel as you and Web never failed to do—relaxed and comfortable. I shall walk home and sleep the rest of the night away, I am sure of it."

She smiled at him as he lowered his head and kissed her lightly on the cheek.

Bruce was in the blackest of moods when Alice arrived at Portman Square the following morning. The physician had been summoned and had given the incredible verdict that Phoebe had indeed succumbed to a case of the measles. She was in bed with a high fever, a sore throat, and a headache.

"It is ridiculous," Bruce said. "A woman of forty does not have the measles." He sounded aggrieved, as if he suspected the doctor of having deliberately given a false diagnosis.

"But clearly it is possible," Alice said calmly. "Poor Phoebe. She must be feeling wretched."

"What about my feelings?" the fond husband replied. "There are the children not half well yet and needing to be taken about for air. And there is Jarvis out until all hours of the night or morning, doubtless making a begger of me at the tailor's and at the gaming tables. And there is Amanda. How am I to go on without Phoebe?"

Alice did not point out that perhaps White's and Brooks' and any other club her brother frequented could probably survive without his constant presence for the next week or so.

"Don't trouble yourself, Bruce," she said. "I shall nurse Phoebe, and Jarvis shall be given the task of taking the children about during the daytime. It will give him something to do, and they will be delighted to have the company of their elder brother. As for

Amanda, I am sure a week of somewhat fewer social activities will not harm her.''

"Phoebe will never recover," he said. "She is burning with fever and worrying over Amanda.''

Alice sighed. She knew quite perfectly what her brother was going to say next.

"There is no choice in the matter," he said. "You will have to take Amanda about, Alice. You are a widow, after all, even if you are rather young. That makes you respectable.''

Alice did not point out that she had been hoping to return to Bath within the week. She did not mention the fact that she had no wish to attend any other social function in London. What was the point? She was a widow and as such could not possibly have anything else of value to do with her life but serve the needs of her brother and his family.

"For a couple of days, then," she said. "Perhaps we will be able to make arrangements with the family of one of Amanda's friends to take her about after that.''

"I would not dream of inconveniencing anyone outside my own family," Bruce said. "I cannot imagine what would make you suggest such a thing, Alice. All I am asking you to do is dress up and enjoy yourself. Anyone would think I was begging you to make some great sacrifice.''

"I shall look in on Phoebe," Alice said, "and then find Amanda to discover what is planned for today.''

It seemed that Amanda had a walk in the park planned for the afternoon with a friend whose mama was unable to accompany them. In the evening there was to be a private concert at the home of Lady Wingham. At least, Alice decided, she would get air and exercise and doubtless hear some good music. At least there would be no dancing that day.

And at least she was unlikely to catch more than a glimpse of Piers as he drove Miss Borden in the park. She very much doubted that he would be at the concert. Although he had liked to hear her play the pianoforte at Chandlos, he had always professed a horror of vocal music.

She did not particularly want to see Piers. What she really wanted to do was return home to her safe and dull and comfortable life in Bath. She could cheerfully shake Phoebe for catching the measles, she thought uncharitably.

Piers had asked her if she found life hard without Web. She had answered truthfully. For though it had been dreadfully hard at first, and though she still found herself storing up some anecdote to tell him or planning to consult him with some problem or decision, she had faced reality after the first few months with a determination not to crumble or draw other people's pity.

It had been a dreadful wrench to have to leave Chandlos, of course. Dreadful to leave the neighborhood where she had always lived and which she had always loved. And yet she had settled to life in Bath with surprising ease and contentment. She loved the city and its activities, and she had formed a pleasing circle of friends and acquaintances. Life was by no means exciting there, but it was very bearable.

And now that had all been upset, or threatened to be upset. She was in London, which she had always found exciting, though Web had not liked to spend much time there. And she had been to a London theater and found it marvelously fascinating and to a London ball and felt like a girl again.

She wanted to stay. She wanted to be a part of it all. And perhaps she would have considered herself wonderfully blessed by circumstances if that were all. For now, whether she liked it or not, she was being forced into the very heart of high society for a few days.

But that was not all. For she was being enticed again by a very old dream, one so old that she had thought it quite incapable of being revived. She had thought it could never bring her pain again.

But it was bringing her pain. And the need to dissemble after all these years of doing so just seemed too much of an effort now.

For several days she would be forced to watch him with younger girls, smiling at them, charming them, choosing which one he would make his bride. And discussing his choice with her and asking her opinion.

And for days she must be his friend, smiling at him and listening to him, laughing at his careless wit, accepting attentions which should be improper but which were not so because they were such very old friends and she knew she had nothing to fear from him. She must accept such brotherly gestures as hands at her waist and kisses on her cheek.

Perhaps she must even waltz with him again and feel the warmth of his closeness and smell the distinctiveness of his cologne.

And when he asked her opinion of his chosen bride, she must try to dissuade him from choosing a girl who could bring him only restlessness and boredom and ultimate unhappiness. And if by chance he chose someone who would be suited to him, she must smile her encouragement.

She must never look into his eyes, her own unmasked, and say, "Choose me, Piers. Choose me!"

Perhaps she could. Perhaps she still had enough youth and beauty. And certainly she had more social significance than when she had been merely Alice Carpenter, the rector's daughter. But she would not. For she had far too much to lose.

She had a friendship to lose that was more dear to her than anything else in her life. A friendship that was agony to continue but that would be a living death to lose.

At the age of fifteen she had begun to train herself to cultivate a friendship where she had longed to entice love. For fourteen years she had held that love only in the deepest, most secret recesses of her being and been his friend with the rest of herself. He had never known. Web had never suspected. And years before she had given up feeling guilty or trying in vain to deny her feelings. For there is no guilt in harboring a forbidden love unless that love sullies or diminishes the affection one should show to a lawful partner.

Web had never suffered from her love for his best friend. Perhaps she had cared for him all the better for having to make her love for him a conscious thing. And she had loved Web. Very, very dearly. Her love for him had had all those ingredients she had listed to Piers the night before. All except one—that last, nameless something that she had only ever felt for Piers himself.

She would die if she lost his friendship, she felt. And yet she longed and longed to be able to flee that friendship in order to return to the dull haven of Bath.

She saw Mary and Richard on their way for a short drive in the barouche with Jarvis after luncheon and returned home to Cavendish Square in order to change into something more appropriate for a walk in the park.

Mr. Bosley was not at home when Mr. Westhaven arrived late in the afternoon to take Cassandra driving, to the latter gentleman's disappointment. He had looked forward to being entertained once more with an account of the man's wealth, his manner of acquiring it, and his hopes of disposing of it.

However, Mr. Bosley had had a talk with his niece before leaving for an afternoon of business in the city.

"So, Cassie," he had said with a rumbling laugh, "you had to sleep the morning away, did you, because you were dancing with all the young dandies all night."

"Everyone was most obliging, Uncle," she said.

He crossed the room in order to pinch her cheek. "For such a pretty puss," he said, "they did not have to exert themselves, I'll wager. And what is this I hear from your mama about bouquets arriving this morning?"

"Mr. Farrell and Mr. Carpenter were obliging enough to send them, Uncle," she said.

"Hm," he said, "I shall look into the prospects of

those gentlemen, Cass. And what of Mr. Westhaven? Did he dance with you?

"Twice, Uncle," she said. "And he led me in to supper."

"He is the one," he said. "He is rich, Cass, which is all to the good since it suggests that he will not waste my blunt when he gets his hands on it. More to the point, he is a member of an old family and has a large and respected estate. That is what counts, Cassie girl. Land. That is what makes a man someone. Your uncle, now, could probably buy up the southern half of England without beggaring himself, but he will never be anyone because he don't have what counts."

Cassandra found no answer to this speech.

"You have to smile at him, Cassie," her uncle said. "Talk to him. Wear your jewels. Make up to him. He'll be yours in a week. Taking you driving this afternoon, is he?"

"Yes, Uncle," she said. "He was kind enough to invite me."

"No kindness in it, Cass," he said. "He is looking for a young bride just like you. All you will be expected to do after your marriage is present him with an heir—or two, for good measure—and then you can enjoy the life of a rich lady for the rest of your days. Have you been exerting yourself to fix his interest?"

"Yes, Uncle," she said.

"But mind, Cassie," he said, winking and beaming at her, "never forget that you are a lady. Never do anything that a lady would not do. He would not like it and might be disgusted with you. No being alone with him or kissing him."

Cassandra pleated the skirt of her dress with her fingers. "No, Uncle," she said.

The girl was dressed in spring green muslin. The brim of her straw bonnet was trimmed with spring flowers that looked for all the world as if they were real except that they did not wilt during the whole of the drive. She looked quite pretty enough to eat.

Indeed, Mr. Westhaven was amused to find that he had acquired many other young male friends since the previous day, if the number who hailed him from horseback or the perches of their curricles was any indication. All of them, of course, after commenting on the unusual felicity of the weather, turned with polite interest to be presented to his companion.

He pursed his lips and considered the strange phenomenon of a girl who spoke scarcely a word and rarely raised her eyes from her lap and yet was as alluring as the most accomplished of the courtesans he had known. If she were not so very shy, he would have wondered if her manner were not all artifice.

She clung to his sleeve as he turned his horses into the park, and then she blushed and apologized.

"You are quite welcome to take my arm if you will feel safer to do so," he said, "though I do assure you I have never been known to overset any of my carriages. You see?" He pointed ahead with his whip. "All the fashionable world is here ahead of us."

She looked timidly about her, and her hand crept to his sleeve again. "Mama and I were so quiet in the country," she said. "I had not expected anything like this."

"Do you prefer the country?" he asked. "I must applaud your taste. Sometimes I long for my own estate, especially at this time of year."

"Oh," she said, raising large eyes to his for a moment, "do you have an estate, sir? How can you bear to leave it?"

"Because," he said, noting the loveliness of her cheeks as her eyelashes fanned down over them again, "life on a large estate for a single gentleman can become very lonely."

"You have no family?" she asked.

"A mother," he said, "who remarried years ago and spends her life in London and Paris. I had a wife and would have had a daughter had she lived. Unfortunately, neither of them did."

He was surprised to see a tear roll from beneath her

lashes. "How very tragic for you," she said. "How very sad you must still be."

"That was almost nine years ago," he said. "And how did the conversation become so morbid? Tell me something of yourself. How did you spend your time in the country?"

But her short burst of conversation had died. She became mute on the subject of herself and so alarmingly shy when other people began to greet them that Mr. Westhaven began to feel his customary amusement again. He felt very much like a protective uncle. And really, he thought, delightful and lovely as she undoubtedly was, how could he feel an attraction to a girl half his age? How could he picture himself standing at the altar with her? Bedding her? Impregnating her with his heir? The very thought was enough to make him want to shout with laughter.

He was delighted to be offered a diversion. There was Allie, looking very smart indeed in dark royal blue, walking with her niece and an unknown young lady. He maneuvered his horses over to them and drew them to a halt. He raised his hat.

"Miss Carpenter?" he said. "Allie? Ma'am? You are putting us to shame, I see, by exercising while we are exercising only the horses. May I present Miss Borden, daughter of the late Lord Margam, and newly arrived in town?"

The presentations were made and a short conversation ensued.

"I saw you last night," Amanda said to Cassandra. "My brother danced with you."

"Mr. Carpenter was obliging enough to send me flowers this morning," Cassandra said.

"Was he?" Amanda laughed. "I shall be sure to tease him about that."

"Oh, pray do not," Cassandra said, distressed.

"Has your sister-in-law recovered, Allie?" Mr. Westhaven asked.

"She has measles," she said, "That is why I am

with Amanda. I am afraid she has to be content with me as chaperon for the next several days.''

''Oh, Aunt Alice,'' the girl said, linking her arm through her aunt's, ''It is vastly more fun to be with you than with Mama. Is it not, Henrietta?''

''That can mean only one thing,'' Mr. Westhaven said. ''It must mean that Allie is more indulgent than your mama, Miss Carpenter. I shall have to find out your papa and advise him of the fact.''

Amanda giggled. ''You would not do so,'' she said. ''Besides, it is not so. It is just that Aunt Alice is so pretty that she turns heads our way.''

Both young ladies giggled.

The horses were restless. ''I shall see you tonight at Lady Wingham's concert, then,'' Mr. Westhaven said with a wink for Alice. ''Until then, be good.''

The two girls giggled again.

Cassandra was clinging to Mr. Westhaven's sleeve again as they resumed their slow drive. He smiled at her.

''Are you all right?'' he asked.

''Oh, yes,'' she said. ''I thank you. It is just that this is so overwhelming. The crowds. But the park is very beautiful.''

''The problem is easily solved,'' he said. ''We will take to a less frequented path, where you may enjoy nature without the crowds.''

''You are most obliging,'' she said. ''I hope it is not improper.''

''Improper?'' he said. ''Absolutely not, Miss Borden, for we will still meet carriages and horses, you know.''

''Thank you,'' she said. ''You are very kind.''

Since her powers of conversation seemed to be exhausted for that day, he set himself to entertain her with a description of all the delights London had to offer.

It had not been a very wise choice of topic, he thought later as he drove home to his lodgings on St. James's Street. Not at least if he did not wish to give the impression that he was singling the girl out for unusual attention. For somehow—he had no idea how—he had suggested taking the girl out to Richmond Park and to Kew Gardens. And he had found himself promising to organize a party to Vauxhall one evening when there were to be fireworks and dancing.

He was going to have to be very careful. For whomever he chose to be his bride before this infernal Season was over, it must not be Miss Cassandra Borden. To say she was a member of the infantry was to understate the case. She was a member of the nursery flock.

He was going to have to get Allie to help him. That was what he was going to have to do. Allie was always sensible. He always felt safe and unthreatened with her.

And he need lose no time before talking to her. He would see her that evening at the concert. He felt more lighthearted and cheerful just at the thought.

# 6

ALICE'S hope was not to be realized, though of course she had known it that afternoon during the brief conversation in the park. Piers was at the concert, she saw as soon as she and Amanda were ushered to their seats. He was making himself agreeable to a young lady and her parents at the other side of the room. All three of them were laughing at something he had just said.

"There is Mr. King," Amanda whispered, taking Alice's arm in an almost painful grip. "The gentleman who danced with me twice last night and who bowed to us from his saddle this afternoon. Don't you think him splendidly fashionable, Aunt Alice?"

"Yes, indeed," Alice agreed. "Do you have a partiality for him, Amanda?"

Her niece groaned in reply. "Oh, he is smiling at me," she said, scarcely moving her lips and smiling and nodding in return. "Just wait until I tell Henrietta."

Alice settled herself to enjoy a recital on the pianoforte and a harp solo. They were to be followed by the main guest for the evening, a soprano who was reputed to have sung to great acclaim in both Vienna and Paris as well as in London.

Mr. King completed Amanda's joy by offering to fetch the ladies lemonade during the interval, and then he settled to conversing with Amanda, who had been joined by another young lady and her brother before his return. Alice watched them, pleased that her niece was enjoying herself.

"Are your eardrums ringing, Allie?" Piers had taken the seat next to hers without her even noticing his approach in the crowded room.

"Ringing?" she said.

"Well, Madame whatever-her-name-is—have you noticed how opera singers always have Italian names?—is a mite screechy, is she not?" he said.

"Your trouble is that you do not appreciate good music," she said. "She has a rather lovely voice, I thought. I am looking forward to the second half."

"So am I," he said. "She may screech, but those deep breaths she takes do wondrous things for her bosom. You aren't blushing again, are you, Allie?"

"I hope you did not make that observation to the young lady you are sitting with," she said. "If you did, I think you may strike one name off your list of prospective brides."

"To Miss Kerns?" he said. "No, no, Allie. What do you think of me? That I do not know how to behave in company?"

"Ah, I see," she said. "I do not qualify as company. Thank you."

He grinned at her. "Not at all," he said. "You qualify as friend. One can say what one wishes to a friend."

"What an alarming thought," she said.

"Especially when one enjoys seeing her blush," he said. "Isn't that something rather new, Allie?"

"Not at all," she said. "It is just that you would not have dared say some of the outrageous things you say to me in front of Web. You know you wouldn't, Piers. He would have reprimanded you."

"Ah," he said. "Just so. I need your help, Allie."

"Do you?" she asked, looking at him warily.

"I seem to have got myself into something of a predicament," he said. "With Miss Borden, that is. She is such a sweet and timid little thing. Don't you think so?"

"I cannot pass judgment," she said. "I have not been enough in her company."

"Ah," he said. "But we can put that right, Allie. The point is that she does see me as a father figure—no, don't look scornful, I swear she does. She clung to my sleeve in the park in the most amusing way, Allie—me, one of the most notable whips in London, even if I do say so myself. And she was terrified of all the young bucks who were making up to her. The long and the short of it is that I suggested taking her about a few times—I particularly mentioned Kew and Richmond and Vauxhall."

"And you are wondering if Mr. Bosley has already drawn up the marriage contract?" she said. "I would not be at all surprised if you are right, Piers."

"I feel the noose tightening about my neck," he said. "Or perhaps it would be more appropriate to say I feel parson's mousetrap pinching my toes or the ball and chain being soldered about my leg."

"And yet," she said, "it was your choice to start looking about you for a bride, Piers."

"Was it really?" he said. "I thought my mother had something to do with it. Though I suppose you are right. She has had little enough influence over me for the last twenty years or so, as she would be the first to tell you."

"You needed my help," she said. "What can I do for you?"

"You can stay close to me," he said. "Come with me wherever I go with Miss Borden."

"Absolutely not!" she said, shocked. "What a totally insane suggestion, Piers. The very idea!"

"Oh, not just you," he said. "I realize that you have to trail along with your niece these days. I am not asking you to abandon her. Bring her along, too. It will seem quite natural for us to try to throw the girls together."

"Like an indulgent uncle and aunt?" she said. "Absolutely not."

"Well, then," he said, "I will organize parties each time. Who is the orange-haired youth with your niece now? A prospective suitor? I shall invite him, too.

And perhaps the giggly chit who was with you this afternoon. I can invite your nephew to accompany her. He is kicking his heels with nothing to do, is he not? Now, does that sound better?''

''And I am to smile benevolently at all these happy couples?'' she said. ''Why did I not stay in Bath?''

''No, no,'' he said. ''I will entertain you, of course, Allie.'' Then he paused and frowned. ''No, that is not right, is it? I will be accompanying Miss Borden. Oh, confound it, I would prefer to be with you. You are far more sensible.''

''Thank you,'' she said. ''That is quite the most delightful compliment you could possibly pay a lady.''

''That she is sensible?'' he said, his eyebrows raised. He looked at her in some surprise. ''And so it is, too. But I have offended you, haven't I? I do assure you I did not mean to. Allie! I enjoy your company more than that of any other lady I have ever known. Pink has never been my favorite color, but you look very fine indeed in that particular shade, I must say.''

She laughed suddenly. ''Flatterer!'' she said.

''I shall invite the oily baronet to escort you, then, shall I?'' he asked. ''Or is there someone you prefer?''

''I do not know anyone else,'' she said. ''And I have agreed to none of this, Piers.''

''You will, though,'' he said, taking one of her hands in his and patting it. ''You are a good sport, Allie, and will not abandon me to my fate. And if Lansing must hang around you, as he surely will, it might as well by in my sight so that I can draw his cork if he tries harassing you.''

''Oh, Piers,'' she said, ''I really do not want to be doing this, you know. And oh dear, the music is about to begin again.''

''Make it easy on yourself,'' he said, circling her wrist with his thumb and forefinger as he had done at the ball the night before. ''Say yes.''

''Ohhh—yes, then,'' she said. ''If I hesitate further, I will probably have you invading my sitting room again tonight and have all my servants resigning to-morrow morning.''

"I could kiss you," he said, getting to his feet and releasing her wrist, "but I won't in so public a setting. Thank you, Allie.''

"My pleasure, Piers," she said, looking at him disapprovingly.

He grinned and winked at her.

Cassandra was dressed from head to toe in primrose yellow as she waited for Mr. Westhaven to come to convey her to Richmond Park.

"Just like a ray of sunshine," her uncle said, beaming at her and rubbing his hands together. "And such a perfect day it is, too, Cass, after the gloom of the past three days. You don't think that the emeralds would match the outfit?''

"Young girls do not wear emeralds, brother," Lady Margam said quickly. "And such jewels are inappropriate for an afternoon outing, anyway.''

"Are they, though?" he said cheerfully. "Well, you should know, Lucinda, having moved about with the nobs since your marriage to Margam. It's a pity, though. I'll wager none of those other chits possess such costly pieces.''

Lady Margam had declined an invitation to join the excursion since she considered Miss Carpenter's widowed aunt chaperon enough. But she had overseen her daughter's preparations, knowing well her brother's tendency to vulgarity. She had already shuddered and assured him that it would not be at all the thing to offer Mr. Westhaven money to take the members of his party out to tea.

"He mentioned a picnic, anyway, brother," she had said.

"Things are coming along very nicely indeed," Mr. Bosley said, continuing to rub his hands in satisfaction. "He is very attentive, Cass. You are following my instructions, are you? Smiling at him and talking to him, fighting your shyness?''

"Yes, Uncle," she said.

"Mind you sit beside him in the carriage," he said. "And take his arm as soon as he hands you down. Dazzle him, Cass. But be sure you stay with the rest of the party, mind." He winked.

"Cassandra would not dream of doing otherwise, brother," Lady Margam assured him.

And so a few minutes later, the girl was sitting in Mr. Westhaven's barouche beside him, blushing becomingly when she found that her knees were almost touching those of an openly admiring Mr. Carpenter sitting opposite. She returned his greeting and that of Miss Marks beside him without raising her eyes. Her hand crept to Mr. Westhaven's sleeve and returned quickly to her own lap. But he lifted it and drew it through his arm, and she darted him a grateful look from beneath her lashes.

The barouche behind Mr. Westhaven's was occupied by Sir Clayton Lansing, Mr. King, Alice, and Amanda. It was a perfect day for a walk and a picnic, they all agreed as the carriages took them beyond the city and out to the spacious park. Before the carriages drew to a halt they were fortunate to pass a herd of grazing deer, which set the girls to squealing with delight and the trigger fingers of some of the gentlemen to itching.

Mr. Westhaven instructed his servants on the setting of the blankets and the disposing of the picnic baskets until they should be ready for tea. His guests in the meantime had begun to stroll across a lawn, exclaiming at the ancient oaks that lined it, relics of the medieval forests of England.

"Well, devil take it," he muttered to himself, amused, as he saw that one of the couples was Miss Borden and Jarvis Carpenter. The other was Amanda Carpenter and Mr. King. Sir Clayton Lansing was conversing politely with Alice and Miss Marks.

"Ah," he said, "it will be delightful to walk after the long drive. Tea will wait for an hour or so. Allie?" He offered her his arm.

''That was rather wicked,'' she said as they walked away, leaving Sir Clayton bowing to Miss Marks.

''Not at all,'' he said. ''Your nephew thinks he has outmaneuvered me. Well, two can play at that game. And you will not deny that you prefer my company to that of the oily baronet, Allie, will you? But perhaps''—he patted her hand as it rested on his arm—''you had better not answer that question. I might find your reply mortifying. Does the infant not shine bright this afternoon?''

''Very,'' she said. ''Jarvis is dazzled, certainly.''

''This works well,'' he said. ''I could not have planned it better. Did you not enjoy Bosley's courtesy in coming from the house, Allie, in order to shake everyone by the hand?''

''I thought it a very pleasant gesture,'' she said.

''Ah,'' he said. ''That was because he admired your bonnet, Allie.''

''And Amanda's pelisse and Miss Marks's parasol,'' she said with a laugh. ''But it was all kindly meant, Piers. You are not going to apologize for his vulgarity, are you, as Sir Clayton did as Mr. Bosley waved us on our way?''

He threw back his head and laughed. ''I would not do so now even if I had intended to,'' he said. ''No, no, Allie, Bosley was worth coming to London for. He is a quite priceless character. You must see to it that you have a free afternoon tomorrow, by the way. How is your sister-in-law?''

''Wallowing in misery and spots,'' she said. ''She really is having a hard time of it, poor Phoebe. And why must I have a free afternoon, pray?''

''I have had a royal summons from my mother,'' he said. ''To tea. She has heard you are in town and directed me to bring you. She must think I have enormous influence with you if she finds it unnecessary to send you a formal invitation. You will come?''

''Yes,'' she said. ''Thank you. I enjoyed seeing your mother last autumn in Bath. Your stepfather was taking the waters.''

"Ah, yes," he said. "The cure-all for a year of overeating."

"You are very unkind," she said. "Sir Barry Neyland is a very amiable gentleman."

"Oh, agreed," he said. "I did not imply that over indulging oneself at the table makes one an unpleasant character, you know. Only an overweight and somewhat unhealthy one. I shall come early for you and we will visit some of the galleries."

"Will we?" she said. "I will enjoy that."

"Yes," he said, "and so will I. You cannot imagine the tedium of taking young ladies about, Allie. One must take them to the Tower to delight them with the animals or awe them with a sight of the crown jewels. Or else to Astley's to see the horses perform. Never to a gallery. It is a pity it is not considered quite the thing for ladies to view the Elgin marbles. I would like to take you there."

"Yes," she said, "I would like to see them."

"Because they are reputed to be magnificent sculptures or because so many of them depict naked men?" he asked, turning his head to look at her as he did so. "Allie, you are crimson."

"And you are no gentleman," she said. "Piers, how dare you."

"Perhaps it is a good thing I cannot take you to see them after all," he said. "Doubtless you would be scarlet down to your toes. No, don't say it. Shall we catch up to your niece and her beau and make ourselves agreeable?"

All eight of them came together for a few minutes and exchanged admiring comments on the scenery and the magnificent weather. Sir Clayton took Cassandra on his arm for the return stroll, while Alice walked with Mr. King, Henrietta Marks with Jarvis, and Amanda with Mr. Westhaven.

A whole hour had passed by the time they returned to the carriages and the blankets, and by mutual consent they decided that it was teatime.

Alice, observing the scene around her, was fascinated to note that the very shy Miss Borden quickly became the focus of almost everyone's attention. Mr. King, it was true, directed all his gallantry to Amanda, to whom he had been paying determined court since the night of the Partiton ball. And Sir Clayton lavished Alice with compliments and loaded a plate with food for her.

But Jarvis was plainly smitten with Cassandra and did his best to draw her into conversation. And Piers sat protectively close to her and focused all his attention on her as if to protect her from her own shyness. He looked a little amused, Alice thought. Indeed, he looked exactly as he had always looked with Harriet.

The foolish man. Despite all his claims that he did not want to commit himself on this relationship, was history about to repeat itself? Would Miss Borden be his bride before the summer was out? It seemed very likely.

Even Sir Clayton seemed to have eyes for no one but the girl during tea.

What was it about her? Alice observed her very closely. Abnormally shy girls, however pretty, usually found themselves left to themselves. There was nothing particularly attractive about shyness. And this girl scarcely had the courage to lift her head or her eyes. She was, of course, very pretty with her masses of auburn ringlets, her flawless complexion, and her very shapely figure.

Was the girl an actress? The idea grew on Alice as tea progressed. She scarcely looked up or spoke, of course, but she communicated quite well enough. A peep from beneath her lashes, a parting of the lips, an almost unobtrusive hand gesture, a slight leaning of the body—toward Piers: all brought an immediate response from one or all of the gentlemen.

The girl positively oozed sensual appeal, Alice decided before tea was finished. And she felt foolish and guilty at the thought. Was she seeing something that simply was not there just because most of the lures seemed to be directed toward Piers? Was she jealous? It was a mortifying thought.

Sir Clayton suggested that they walk in the rhododendron gardens after tea. Everyone was willing, the afternoon being still bright and warm. But Cassandra was turned to Mr. Westhaven, looking up at him briefly and thanking him for the tea. Sir Clayton turned to offer his arm to Alice.

"My dear Mrs. Penhallow," he said. "Pray, do me the honor."

She smiled and took his arm. They led the way among the blooms, admiring them and smelling them until she was aware after twenty minutes that there were only three couples proceeding along the walks between the tall bushes. Piers and Miss Borden were nowhere in sight.

He supposed he could do a great deal worse, Mr. Westhaven thought as he took Miss Borden on his arm and followed the others to look at the rhododendrons. He would certainly be the envy of a large portion of the male population of London, Jarvis Carpenter, for example. And even Lansing, despite his continued fawning over Allie.

What he should do was marry her without giving himself time to think about the matter. He did not believe she would be averse to the match, despite what she had said to him on that first evening at the theater. Indeed, she seemed to favor him even over the far younger Carpenter.

He should offer for her, marry her, install her at Westhaven Park, get her with child, and then know that his main duty to this infernal new position of his was done. It would not be a bad marriage. She would doubtless be good to look at for years to come, and she would not interfere with his main pleasures: reading and riding and overseeing his lands when he was at home. Indeed, she seemed to be a girl who would be eager to please.

"Oh," she said now, "this reminds me of home.

The lovely smells of home.'' Her voice was filled with longing.

"Does it?'' he said. ''Is it not strange how smell can evoke memories more than any other sense?''

She was not unlike Harriet, except that Harriet had not been quite as shy. Indeed, she had liked to chatter on occasion, though she had been awed to silence by his mother, and by Web and Allie, though they had tried their best to set her at her ease. But there was a likeness—a similarity in size and form, a sweetness, a childlike innocence.

Harriet had been very sweet. He had married her on a whim because he could not bear the thought of going home alone again. But he had grown fond of her. And he had felt all the responsibility of knowing that she was deeply in love with him.

Poor Harriet.

But did he want to repeat that sort of relationship? The necessity of conversing with his wife as he would with a child? The inability to share any of his inner self with her?

The boredom?

But did it matter? Was life that exciting anyway? At least if he married and had children, he would satisfy his mother and Lord Berringer. And himself, too. He thought he would rather enjoy having sons of his own. And daughters, too. Perhaps especially daughters.

"Am I walking a little fast for you?'' he asked the girl now, bending his head to hers as he noticed the gap between them and the others widening.

"Oh, no,'' she said. ''I am just enjoying the flowers so much.''

And how could one not feel drawn to a child who admired flowers? he thought with a wave of inner amusement.

Of course, there was always the other side of the coin, the side that had made him restless for days, ever since he had invited himself up to Allie's sitting room after the Partiton ball. There was always the knowledge of what marriage should be in its ideal form.

She had described it for him. A certain magic, she had called it. He could scoff at what she had said, and indeed he did. She had described perfection, and perfection is impossible to achieve in this life.

Or so he would have thought if he had not himself been witness to such a perfect marriage—Allie's own. Being with them had always filled him with a yearning for a similar sort of love. He had tried to find it, but he had never come close.

Perhaps he might have if he had not been preoccupied for so many years by his own infatuation with Allie. It had always seemed unfair to him that Web had confided his love for her when she was fifteen before he had thought to confide his own. He and Web had been like brothers. He had found himself unwillingly to risk their friendship by competing for the same girl.

Perhaps it was the knowledge that she was beyond him that had made his love of her such a lasting, painful thing. Her wedding day had been one of the most agonizing days of his life.

He had continued to love her for several years—she was the reason he had married Harriet so precipitately and the reason he had been torn with such guilt on Harriet's death—even though he knew that he could never have won her. Web would have won that contest if there had been one. For Web had been steady and kindly and a gentleman in every sense of the word. He had been worthy of Allie, if anyone could possibly be so.

His own love had been sublimated into friendship. There was no point in blighting one's whole life, he had persuaded himself eventually with unaccustomed good sense, over a woman who was as far beyond him as the sun and the moon.

She was his dearest friend now. No more than that. But if he let himself think too deeply, he could still dream of finding someone like her, but someone he was worthy of, someone who could share his life with him as Allie has shared hers with Web.

That was the other side of the coin. It was not worth turning the coin over to see. If he was to marry and have children, then he must choose a bride soon without being foolish enough to dream that perhaps at the age of six-and-thirty he would find that one woman who would suddenly be the meaning of his whole life.

He was jolted back to reality and to a realization of his ill-mannered silence by the sight of Miss Borden fumbling in a pocket and bringing out a small lace-edged handkerchief. She sniffed. Good Lord, she was crying!

"What is it?" he asked gently, taking the handkerchief from her hand and wiping away her tears. The others, he noticed with a quick glance, were out of sight. Where was Allie when he most needed her?

"It is nothing," she said, her voice vibrating on a sob. "It is nothing at all."

Had he drawn her into his arms or had she come there? But there she was, sobbing on his chest. He held her close, patting his hand soothingly against her back.

"Oh, forgive me," she said eventually. "Pray forgive me."

"But what is it?" he asked, lowering his head to hers. "Is it something I have said or done?"

"N-no," she said. "Oh, nothing, sir. It is just the rhododendrons."

"The rhododendrons?" he said.

"They remind me so of home," she said. "Of the country. And I fear I will never be back in the country again. Mama and Uncle want to find me a husband, and I fear he will be a man who will live always in London. And I do not think I could bear it. Though I cannot disappoint Mama and Uncle."

Oh, Lord. Mr. Westhaven looked hopefully down the path again, willing Alice to appear. This needed a woman's touch. The path was empty.

"But you will have choices," he said. "You are a very pretty young lady, and you must have noticed the interest various gentlemen have shown in you already.

I am sure your mother will not try to force you to marry one particular gentleman. She will want your happiness.''

''But Uncle wishes to choose my husband,'' she said. ''And he has lived all his life in town. Oh, what am I to do?''

''Dry your eyes and blow your nose for a start,'' he said. ''I shall take you back to the carriages then, shall I? You will have time to compose yourself before the others return. And why do you not tell your mama just what you have told me? Surely she will understand.''

''Yes,'' she said. ''I am so sorry, sir. I am so very sorry. I feel quite humiliated to have shown my feelings thus. I wish we had not come this way.''

''So do I,'' he said, ''if it distresses you so. Come now, smile at me. All will turn out well for you, you will see. Are you to be at the Hendon ball tomorrow evening? You must reserve the opening set for me, if you will. And I shall organize the night at Vauxhall that I promised. You cannot fail to enjoy yourself there and forget all your woes.''

She did peep up at him very briefly with a look of melting gratitude. But he had never seen her smile, he realized with sudden interest.

''You are very kind,'' she said. ''So very kind, sir. I am so glad I was with you. I am sure no one else would understand. They would have been impatient with me. But you are from the country. You understand how I feel.''

''Yes, certainly I do,'' he said, taking her hand within his arm again and patting it. He turned back toward the carriages and walked as fast as he felt he decently could. They had been alone quite long enough.

# 7

PHOEBE, having withdrawn from the social scene with the greatest reluctance, now showed an equal unwillingness to return to it. She complained of continued symptoms of her illness and insisted on lying in bed all day in a darkened room. Although Alice sat with her for a half hour the morning after the picnic, trying to take her sister-in-law's mind off herself by describing in detail Amanda's successes of the previous few days, clearly it was an impossible task.

Mary and Richard were up and about, though Mary was still peevish and clearly irritated that her mother had taken some attention away from her. Amanda was very weary and quite content to spend the day at home, with the exception of a quick trip to Bond Street with Henrietta Marks and her mama late in the morning. She declared her intention of resting all afternoon so that she might be able to enjoy the Hendon ball in the evening.

"Do you like Mr. King?" she asked Alice, frowning in thought.

"He is a very amiable young man," Alice said.

"You do not think his hair just a little too red?" the girl asked.

Alice was left to conclude that poor Mr. King, who had been enormously fascinating as long as he might not have been interested in Amanda, was seen to have shortcomings now that he had demonstrated that he was.

"But he does have a lovely smile," Amanda added.

Alice looked forward to the afternoon's outing despite herself. It would be lovely, she thought, to be responsible for no one but herself for a few hours. And Piers was always good company. Since it appeared that circumstances were forcing her into his company for a few days, she might as well enjoy it. It was foolish to tell herself that his presence in her life made her restless. It also exhilarated her. She might as well enjoy the exhilaration while she was able.

The summer and winter in Bath would doubtless be long and dull enough.

She was ready to leave before Piers arrived, and dressed in a new dark green dress and matching pelisse. It was a chilly day and raining outside.

The thing was, she thought as she paced the downstairs salon, unable to sit down and relax, she must treat the relationship as a pleasant friendship, as she had trained herself to do through many years. She must know clearly in her mind that this enforced closeness would continue for only a few more days, and then normal life would resume.

There was nothing so terrible in the thought. It had always been so. She had always looked forward to his coming home, but she had never minded dreadfully his leaving again, because her everyday life had been very pleasant. And it still was, even though a great emptiness had been left where Web had been. She had her home in Bath and her friends. She was looking forward in particular to seeing Andrea Potter again.

Yes, she decided, hearing a carriage draw up outside the house, it was entirely possible to take a sensible approach to life. She had grown expert at it through the years.

And then Piers was there at the door of the salon, disdaining the assistance of the servants as he always did, grinning at her, raindrops spotting the shoulders of his coat. Alice smiled.

"Hello, Allie," he said. "I am glad to see you are ready to go. I half expected that you would be huddled close to a fire, afraid of being drowned if you ventured outside. I might have known you were made of sterner stuff.''

"I have already been to Portman Square this morning," she said.

"Of course," he said. "Doubtless you would be expelled from the family if you failed to show up there daily. You do look fine, Allie. Are you spending all of Web's fortune on Bond Street modistes?''

"That is not at all a proper question," she said. "But yes, I have been doing some shopping. I am in London so rarely."

"I thought we might go to the Egyptian Hall on Piccadilly," he said, "and then to Somerset House to see the paintings. Will that suit you?''

"It sounds wonderful to me," she said, passing through the doorway ahead of him as he held the door open for her. "Is the Egyptian Hall where Napoleon Bonaparte's carriage is on display?''

He opened an umbrella at the front door and held it over her head as they hurried to his waiting carriage. "That is my sole reason for taking you there," he said. "You cannot say you have lived a full life until you have seen old Bony's carriage, now can you, Allie?''

"My feelings exactly," she said, settling herself on the seat and shaking the raindrops from her skirt. "I shall be the envy of all my acquaintances in Bath.''

They drove in companionable silence for a few minutes. And then he turned to her impulsively.

"I did a rather foolish thing again yesterday," he said.

"Again?" she said, smiling. She did not know if he realized that he had reached across the space between them and taken her hand in his. She guessed not. But she would not draw his attention to the fact by trying to remove it.

"I reserved the first set at tonight's ball with Miss Borden," he said. "Foolish in the extreme, was it not? I danced the opening set with her at the last ball.''

"Doubtless Mr. Bosley will have the marriage contract ready for your signature the very next time you call on him,'' she said.

He grimaced. ''You don't have to make a joke of it, you know, Allie,'' he said. ''You are permitted to be sympathetic. The whole of the *ton* will be consulting their *Morning Post*s, looking for the announcement.''

''You do not want to marry her?'' she asked.

He sat back in the corner of the carriage and drew her hand onto his lap. ''I feel a decided urge to loosen my cravat,'' he said, ''and to run a cool finger along beneath it. I feel a strange compulsion to don my most comfortable footgear and start running in the direction of Wales or Scotland. I feel the noble instinct to become an ambassador to the court of the sultan of Arabia. Have I answered your question?''

She was laughing. ''And is it just Miss Borden who inspires these feelings in you?'' she asked.

He stared at her without answering for a few moments. ''Oh, Lord, no,'' he said. ''It's the whole infantry regiment, Allie. The whole of the female species. I am terrified. Do you think my mother will disown me as a son if I fail to make a grandmama of her within the next five years or so?''

''I really have no idea,'' she said. ''But why did you ask Miss Borden for the opening set if you feel as you do?''

''Oh, Lord, I don't know,'' he said, smoothing the forefinger of his free hand absently along her fingers. ''She is so very sweet and helpless, Allie. I had the poor chit sobbing in my arms while the rest of you were sedately admiring the rhododendrons. It was as much as I could do to stop myself from kissing her. That would not have been at all the thing with such a very young lady, now, would it?''

''Not with your fear of marriage,'' she said. ''But what happened?''

''She was crying over the flowers,'' he said. ''They reminded her of the country, where she fears she will never live again. It seems that Bosley has some town dandies in mind for her. Poor little girl. She has the tenderest heart, Allie.''

''Does she?'' she said. ''I suppose she knows you have property in the country?''

''Oh, yes,'' he said. ''Anyway, I advised her to talk to her mama. The woman seems sensible enough. Not a dragon, anyway. And I asked her to reserve the opening set for me tonight.''

Alice opened her mouth to speak, but closed it again. It really was not her business to voice suspicions which might well be unfounded.

''Well,'' he said, ''perhaps I will survive the ordeal unscathed after all. And if I don't, then perhaps it will be as well to be forced into something I really ought to do.''

''Marry?'' she said. ''I cannot see that marriage should ever be entered into as a duty, Piers. It is such a very personal commitment.''

''Ah,'' he said, raising her hand to his lips and smiling at her before releasing it, ''but you were very fortunate, Allie. Or perhaps it would be more accurate to say that Web was very fortunate.''

''Yes, that is true,'' she said. ''We both were. But it was a marriage of two human beings anyway, Piers. We had to work at making it a success every day of our lives. It was no easy matter even though we entered into it from personal inclination. I shudder at the thought of a marriage of convenience.''

''And yet you are such a very sensible person,'' he said.

''But it does not make good sense to marry someone just because one feels one ought,'' she said, ''or because one feels that one should produce heirs. The whole of one's life is affected when one marries. One spends one's days with one's spouse, not with one's children. Oh, Piers, you must know the truth of what I say. You were married yourself for more than a year.''

''Yes, so I was,'' he said. ''And so I might still be if things had turned out differently. And I might be papa to a brood, too. I wonder if I would be happier or less happy than I am now. It is impossible to say, is it not? Can you imagine me the father of a brood, Allie?'' He grinned at her.

''Yes, I can,'' she said. ''You would be a good father.'' She turned to look out the window onto the rain-soaked street.

''And you should have been a mother,'' he said. ''I remember how you glowed with Nicky and were quite unwilling to leave him to a nurse's care. But I should not speak as if it were a present impossibility. Are you going to marry again, Allie? You should, you know, provided it is not to the oily baronet, that is. I am sorry I lost sight of you yesterday afternoon, by the way. He did not molest you, did he?''

''No,'' she said, laughing. ''We were well chaperoned, remember.''

''Ah, yes,'' he said. ''I was just afraid that amid those heady blooms he would have waxed romantic and tried to kiss you. He didn't, did he?''

''No, not again,'' she said.

''Again?'' He frowned at her. ''You mean he has before?''

''The night he proposed to me,'' she said, laughing. ''I managed to fight him off.''

''The devil!'' he said. ''I ought to slap a glove in his face. And I would, too, Allie, if half the world would not hear of it and soon know the cause. I shall certainly advise him that he would be safer away from London, if you wish.''

She continued to laugh. ''He fancies himself in love,'' she said, ''and has made me an honorable offer of marriage. That is hardly the occasion for a death threat, Piers.''

''Certainly it is when the lady is you,'' he said. ''The very thought of anyone's mauling you around as if you were a milkmaid!''

''Is this the Egyptian Hall?'' she asked, looking out through the window again.

"The very place," he said. "Bullock's Museum. Let us go and see what is to be seen."

Alice enjoyed the next couple of hours more than anything else since her arrival in London, first there and then at the Royal Academy in Somerset House. Apart from a few jokes about Emperor Napoleon's carriage, Piers was serious and quiet. He did not seem to feel the necessity to comment and exclaim upon everything they saw. And so she was able to become absorbed in the beauty of the paintings.

They stood for a whole hour in Somerset House, gazing at walls covered with canvases. And until she thought about it, it did not seem at all unnatural when a party of schoolboys invaded the room to have Piers encircle her waist with one arm and draw her protectively against his side. He appeared to do so quite unconsciously and continued to gaze upward.

She relaxed against him and did not try to pull away even after she had realized that it was not quite proper to stand thus even if he had been her husband. But there was a sweet, seductive feeling of comfort and closeness, with no unease at all. She found that she could even turn her attention back to the paintings and continue to enjoy them.

He smiled down at her after a while, his arm still about her. "Are you still there?" he asked. "I must be an insufferably dull companion, Allie. I don't think I have uttered a word in the past half hour, have I?"

"But then, neither have I," she said. "Talking seems superfluous when there is so much to see, does it not?"

"Ah, Allie," he said, "you are so peaceful to be with. How do you do it? With everyone else I feel the constant necessity to make noise, however meaningless."

"Perhaps because I am a friend," she said, smiling up at him. Finally she was uncomfortably aware of his nearness, of his arm about her waist, his shoulder brushing her cheek.

"I wish you did not live in Bath," he said. "I wish

you were still at Chandlos or at least in the village. How dare you move away without my permission, Allie." He was laughing at her.

The party of schoolboys had moved on long ago. There was only a pair of ladies at the other side of the room, examining a painting at very close range.

"I know," he said. "Your memories were too painful for you to stay there. That was the real reason, was it not? I'm sorry, Allie. I wish more than anything in the world that I could bring him back for you."

She watched in shock as his head moved the small distance that separated them and he kissed her warmly and lightly on the lips.

"Time to obey that royal summons," he said, releasing her and offering his arm. "I shall be in Mama's black book for the next decade if I am five minutes late producing you for tea."

"That would never do," she said, taking his arm and smiling at him.

Lady Neyland, formerly Mrs. Westhaven, had moved away from Westhaven Park as soon as her son reached his majority, and had remarried very soon after. She and Sir Barry had lived in London or Paris ever since.

However, Alice could remember her from her childhood and knew her from occasional visits into the country since. And she had spent some evenings in company with both her and her husband in Bath the previous year. She liked Piers' mother.

"Piers," Lady Neyland said when they were shown into her drawing room, offering her cheek for his kiss, "you are five minutes late. I said four o'clock. Mrs. Penhallow, my dear, do come and sit down. Is the weather not dreadful?"

But Alice found her hand in the large, hearty clasp of Sir Barry before she was able to take her seat. Piers was explaining to his mother that traffic had been slow and heavy on the streets because of the rain.

"Of course," Lady Neyland said, "and you should

have made allowances for that, Piers. You are no green boy. I hope you have an umbrella for Mrs. Penhallow.''

''Yes, indeed, Mama,'' he said. ''And chased behind her with it from carriage to house so that not a single drop of moisture was allowed to water her bonnet. You see, I am not such a careless creature as you think.''

''It is a great wonder you remembered it,'' she said. ''Your valet must have reminded you. Is it still Vaughan? An excellent man, Vaughan. Doubtless he has prevented you a dozen times from leaving your rooms without your head fixed firmly on your shoulders. Do sit down, Piers. One gets a crick in one's neck from looking up at you.''

''How do you do, sir?'' Piers said to his stepfather, exchanging a wink with him over his mother's head and grinning at Alice.

''I was fine, my boy,'' Sir Barry replied mournfully, ''until your mama put me on half rations.''

''The very idea!'' his wife exclaimed, seating herself behind the teapot and beginning to pour. ''One hates to be vulgar in front of guests, my love, but the truth of the matter is, Mrs. Penhallow, that I have insisted he reduce his rations to double instead of triple what they should be.''

''Sometimes,'' Piers said, stretching out his booted feet to the hearth, where a warm fire was crackling, ''life seems hardly worth living, does it, sir?''

''If it were not for billiards,'' Sir Barry said, ''I might consider shooting myself, m'boy. I am waiting for your mama to conceive the notion that stooping over a cue increases one's girth.''

''I would not say that aloud, if I were you,'' Piers said. ''You might give her ideas.''

''Mrs. Penhallow,'' Lady Neyland said, ''you must be a saint to have entertained my son as often as you apparently did when dear Webster was still alive. Make yourself useful, Piers, do, and take Mrs. Penhallow her tea and the plate of cakes.''

"Allie likes them oozing with cream," he said with a grin, getting to his feet.

"Piers!" she said.

"Now," Lady Neyland said, "you must tell us how our friends in Bath were going along when you left them, Mrs. Penhallow, if you will. And after tea we will send the men packing for a game of billiards, and you must tell me who your modiste is. That is a very becoming outfit. A lovely color. But then I daresay your sense of style is your own and no modiste's at all. I wish I shared your eye for what will suit one."

"How did you leave Mr. and Mrs. Potter?" Sir Barry asked. "Well, I hope?"

Lady Neyland was as good as her word. After a half hour of tea and general conversation, she ordered her husband and son to go and enjoy themselves in the billiard room while she and Mrs. Penhallow had some sensible conversation.

"Men are so like children," she said fondly when the door had closed behind them. "They have to be told what to do or they will never think of it for themselves. But then I do not need to tell you that when you were married for several years. Though I must say that Webster seemed a great deal more sensible than most other men I have ever known."

Alice smiled and let her hostess talk.

"Take Piers, for example," she said. "It is as clear as the nose on your face that he needs a wife. He is restless and bored and lonely, too. And yet he cannot realize it for himself and set about the task of looking about him for a suitable bride. Will you have another cup of tea, my dear? I believe it is still warm."

Alice declined and watched Lady Neyland fill her own cup.

"I had to tell him," her hostess said. "One does not like to tell one's thirty-six-year-old son such a thing, especially when it is quite within his nature to laugh at me and wink at his stepfather over my head as he did earlier, thinking I do not know. He is a horrid, undutiful boy, Mrs. Penhallow, though quite the dearest boy in his fond mama's eyes, of course.''

She sipped her tea and pulled a face. ''Too strong,'' she said. ''I used the death of those poor unfortunate boys as an excuse, and told Piers that he owed it to his new position to get himself married and some children into his nursery. I have been amazed to hear that he has been taking me seriously.''

''He has been diligently attending all the entertainments of the Season,'' Alice said.

''And eyeing all the new little girls who are half his age, so I hear,'' Lady Neyland said. ''What a ridiculous boy. Perhaps no one has told him that women are able to breed well past the age of eighteen. How does he expect to find a mate among the little girls?''

Alice did not think a reply was called for. She smiled.

''Exactly,'' her hostess said, as if Alice had given the wisest of replies. ''He does not have any idea how to go on, Mrs. Penhallow. He never did. You knew Harriet. The sweetest little creature one could ever wish to meet, and she doted on Piers. But I was horrified when I was first presented to her. I can never quite quell the thoroughly nasty thought that he had a fortunate escape from that marriage. He would have been dreadfully unhappy with her by now. Don't you agree?''

Alice hesitated. ''He was very kind to her,'' she said.

''Well, of course he was,'' the other said. ''And doubtless would have continued to be. It is not in Piers' nature to be cruel to people who are weaker than he. But he would have been unhappy. Piers is an intelligent boy, though one would not always think so from the foolish way he likes to talk. He needs a woman whose mind can match his own. Someone like you, for example.'' She took another sip of the tea and then set it firmly in its saucer with a look of extreme distaste.

''Like me?'' Alice said.

Lady Neyland sighed. "He was very fond of you and Webster," she said. "I can remember thinking even when you were still married that it would have been far better for Piers if he had been the one to marry you. I suppose he had the same chance to woo you as Webster had when you were at the rectory with your papa. He could finally settle down if he would but marry someone like you, I believe."

Alice licked dry lips. "But I am not in search of a husband, ma'am," she said.

"No, I know, my dear," Lady Neyland said. "You have been widowed for only two years, and it is hard to risk a second marriage when the first was a happy one, is it not? I had a happy marriage with Mr. Westhaven. It was all of five years before I could contemplate taking another partner."

"I value my independence," Alice said.

"Yes," her hostess said, "I could see that when we were at Bath. You need not look so aghast, my dear. I am not going to push a match on either you or Piers. While you would undoubtedly be good for him, I am not at all sure he would be good for you. He is a careless boy who would not treat you nearly as worshipfully as Webster did. He would as like try to shock you every day of your life merely for the pleasure of watching you blush."

"He does that now," Alice found herself saying with a smile of amusement.

"Then you know what I mean," the other said. "Well, Mrs. Penhallow, my dear, perhaps I have started something that I ought not to have started at all. For a poor marriage will surely be more disastrous for Piers than no marriage at all. Is there anyone special?"

Alice hesitated. "I do not believe his feelings are engaged with anyone," he said. "He has paid attentions to Miss Borden, daughter of Lady Margam, but I think more out of an instinct to protect her from shyness than out of any serious intent to woo her."

"And I suppose she and her mama, as well as every

other girl and her mama, know that he is wealthy and landed and in search of a bride?'' she said dryly.

''I believe so, ma'am,'' Alice said.

Lady Neyland clucked her tongue. ''Piers thinks he is awake on every suit,'' she said. ''But in matters of the heart—or in matters of matrimony, I should say, which is not at all necessarily the same thing—he can be the veriest babe. The chances are that he will end up marrying not the girl he has chosen, but the one who has laid the most careful trap. Am I right, Mrs. Penhallow?''

''I really could not say, ma'am,'' Alice said.

''No, of course you could not,'' Lady Neyland said. ''It would not be proper for you to comment, would it? I should not have asked you. Now I have to decide what to do. Keep my mouth shut, I suppose. For if I talk to him, he will become stubborn and walk into the trap that much sooner. Well, my dear, I still have not asked you about your modiste. This is a London creation, is it not?''

They talked fashions for the time that remained before they were rejoined by the gentlemen.

# 8

He was just simply not going to do it, Mr. Westhaven decided that evening at the Hendon ball. Allie had been right. There had to be more to marriage than just the breeding of heirs. There was more. There was the living with one's mate for the rest of one's life. And if he married a girl half his age, then there was every chance that she would outlive him. He would be taking on a life sentence indeed.

He was finding the evening tedious in the extreme. Dancing with Miss Borden brought no stimulation to the mind, unless one called searching about in one's brain for some topic of conversation that would draw a word or a smile from her stimulating. It was mildly amusing, of course, to try to coax her into peeping up through her lashes at him or even looking directly at him. But would the amusement pall after a few years?

The word seemed to be out that he was paying serious court to Miss Borden. The other mamas and their daughters laid even more determined siege to his heart than usual. It was all vastly entertaining. But after all, he decided, he did not want the inner privacy of his life permanently invaded.

The whole of the social scene was beginning to pall on him. There was, he was discovering, only a certain range of human foolishness to be observed. He had observed it all during the past several weeks. Things were becoming repetitive.

He felt a sudden longing to be back in the country, back at Westhaven. He had not been there for a whole year. He had avoided it, and still did not fancy going there, knowing that strangers were at Chandlos, knowing that he would never be able to ride or stroll there again and find himself more perfectly at home than he had ever been anywhere else in his life.

But Westhaven Park was still home, and he longed for the peace of it, away from the follies of town. And sooner or later he must accustom his mind finally to the knowledge that Web was dead and Allie making a new life for herself in Bath. She would always be his friend, he believed, but he must learn to realize that she could not always be there for him as she had been when she had been at Chandlos.

Yes, he had made up his mind. He just would not do it.

"I am not going to do it, you know," he told Alice when he waltzed with her some time before supper.

"Am I to praise your decision or chide?" she said, raising her eyebrows and smiling up at him. "What is it you are not going to do, Piers?"

"Marry," he said. "I have decided to go to my grave a confirmed bachelor. Or a confirmed widower, I suppose I should say."

"Half of London will go into mourning," she said. "The female half, that is. The male half will probably cheer your withdrawal from the lists."

"Ah," he said, "you choose to laugh at me, Allie. You have become quite saucy lately. I suppose my mother will disown me. She will never have the experience of being a grandmama."

"Am I permitted to ask what has caused this change in plan?" she asked.

"You have," he said, and watched the smile arrested in her eyes for a moment. "You talked sense into me, Allie. Are you not pleased?"

"Yes if I have prevented you from making a disastrous marriage," she said. "No if I have condemned you to a life of loneliness."

"I am going to go back to Westhaven," he said. "I wish I could leave tomorrow now that I have conceived the idea, but I cannot, confound it. I have promised to organize a party to Vauxhall for Miss Borden. Some time next week, I think, and then I shall be free to be on my way.''

"How I envy you," she said.

"Do you?" He grinned at her. "Then come with me. Be my guest. The house is large enough."

"Piers!" she said, laughing. "The very idea. The whole neighborhood would disown you."

"It would not be a good idea anyway, would it?" he said, his smile softening. "I imagine it would be hard on you to be a guest at Westhaven and to know that you did not belong at Chandlos any longer. And to know that Web is not there. Even I find that hard to face."

"But I am glad you are going home," she said. "You are missed there, I am sure. I hope to return to Bath soon, too."

"But not before the Vauxhall night," he said. "I need you there for moral support, Allie. And you must promise me before you leave that you will never marry Lansing."

She laughed. "I promise," she said. "Only because you insist, Piers, but I promise."

"He danced the last set with Miss Borden," he said, "and has signed her card for the supper dance. Perhaps he plans to run off with her and the fishy fortune, Allie. Perhaps you will be safe from him after all."

"I don't think Mr. Bosley's fortune will be a lure to Sir Clayton," she said. "He is reputed to be very wealthy indeed. Do you realize what you have forced me to give up, Piers?"

"I was ever a killjoy," he said.

"You must always remember, Cassie," Mr. Bosley was explaining to his niece at luncheon the next day. Lady Margam was lying down with a headache. "A business head is a cool head. You will gain nothing if you allow yourself to be seduced by appearances."

Cassandra toyed with the food on her plate.

"Mr. Carpenter is a young man and a good-looking one, too, at a guess. Eh, am I right?" he asked.

"Yes, Uncle," she said.

"And so you agreed to drive in the park with him this afternoon," he said. "It is very understandable, Cass. He is young and you are young. But he is a relative nobody, girl. His father owns a small property and has a fortune so modest that only the upper classes would call it a fortune at all. Not that that would matter if he were somebody, of course. But he has nothing to offer you."

"No, Uncle," she said.

"Your mother was moving in the right direction when she married your papa," he said. "But in those days I was in no position to help with the blunt. Now I am, Cassie. You can do as well as your mama and better—and have the money to live on as well."

"Yes, Uncle," she said.

"Westhaven is the one," he said. "I have inquired about all the others who have shown interest in you, Cassie. Not one of them will do at all. Your mother mentioned that Sir Clayton Lansing danced with you twice last evening."

"Yes, Uncle," she said.

"And he was part of the group that went to Richmond, was he not?" he asked.

"Yes, Uncle," she said. "He was obliging enough to walk with me there."

"Hm," he said. "I shall have to make inquiries. In the meantime, Cassie, you must keep making up to Westhaven. You are doing so?"

"He is very attentive, Uncle," she said.

"And still planning to take you to Vauxhall?" he asked.

"Yes," she said. "He said he would call on Mama to make arrangements for next week."

"Good girl," he said. "You must attach him there, girl. A very romantic spot is Vauxhall. You must daz-

zle him and flirt with him. Just make sure you are
never alone with him, Cass." He winked at her.

"Yes, Uncle," she said.

Phoebe was finally recovering from her sickness,
though she felt very weak still, she assured Alice when
the latter mentioned her plan to return home to Bath
the following week. Far too weak to accompany
Amanda everywhere and look after Mary, who was
still peevish.

It was a strange weakness, Alice thought with some
amusement a few days after Phoebe had mentioned it.
It did not at all impede her doing what she wished to
do, like chaperoning Amanda at balls and the livelier
parties. Nor did it stop her from indulging in daily
shopping trips. But it did have her wilting over the
prospect of accompanying her daughter to concerts and
the opera. And it certainly prevented her from taking
her younger daughter about.

That fell to Alice's lot. She took Mary to St. Paul's
and Westminster Abbey, to the New Mint and Madame
Tussaud's. And she talked to the child and tried to think
of other amusements, though she was not very familiar
with London herself. She hid her irritation with her
brother, who spent his life complaining of how his family inconvenienced him and yet never did anything for
their entertainment. Jarvis, to give him his due, was
making some effort to keep Richard amused.

It was Piers who reminded her of the Tower of London and Astley's Amphitheater. He asked her, at the
opera one evening, if she would care to visit the Brit-
ish Museum with him the following afternoon.

"I will try to steer you away from the dustiest sec-
tions," he said.

But she told him with a smile that she had promised
to take Mary for an outing.

"I'll come with you," he said after suggesting the
two possible destinations. "I will enjoy visiting them
again."

"Liar!" she said. "You complained to me only the

other day, Piers, that you get tired of having to take young ladies to those very places."

"Did I?" he said. "I must have been in a vile mood, was I? But you see, Allie, it is the company that makes all the difference."

"You like Mary, then," she said.

"Good Lord," he said. "Do I know her? Actually I like her aunt. Shall we take my curricle and squeeze the child in between us?"

"I am quite sure she would be thrilled," Alice said. "Jarvis flatly refuses to take her up in his, claiming that he would be the laughingstock to be seen driving a child about London in such a sporting vehicle."

"Ah," he said. "Now you tell me. So I am to be the laughingstock, am I? You know, Allie, I have the most ferocious headache. Don't you suppose the composer of this opera might have done us all a kindness by killing off the soprano in the first half instead of waiting until the very last scene?"

"Then there would not have been any point in having a second half to the opera," she said sensibly.

He grinned. "That is good point," he said before sauntering back to join his own party for the remainder of the evening.

Mary was on her best behavior the following afternoon and far more goodnatured than usual. She was cheered by the prospect of being driven about London in the curricle of a gentleman whom her sister had described as very fashionable and her older brother as top-of-the-trees.

They went to the Tower on that first day and looked at the crown jewels and the armory and at the wild animals.

"Though there are not too many of them left," Mr. Westhaven explained. "What they lack in numbers they make up for in ferocity, of course." And he went on to give a lurid account of occasions when the bars of the cages had been gnawed through by the ferocious animals and all the spectators had been gobbled up.

"Pooh," Mary said, "those people were foolish not

to run as soon as the animals started to bite at the bars.''

"But when they are really in a fierce mood," he said, "they can snap their bars in the twinkling of an eye. I don't quite like the look of the gleam in the lion's eye, do you, Allie?"

"How silly you are," Mary said. But Alice was amused to note that her hand had crept into Piers' clasp. The lion looked rather as if it were about to nod off to sleep, she thought.

"They always rest before they attack," Mr. West-haven continued. "Just as the lion is doing now. And the bear. The elephant, of course, can remove the bars of his cage merely by wrapping his trunk about them. It would be most interesting to see, don't you think, Allie?"

"I think perhaps we should move on to see the birds," Alice said, "before Mary's knees buckle under her."

"Oh," the child said scornfully, "I know Mr. Westhaven is just funning us, Aunt Alice."

"Oh, here it comes," he said as the lion exerted itself to lift its head and yawn. "Hold on to me, ladies." And he wrapped an arm about each and hugged them to him, while Mary gave a little shriek.

"Piers!" Alice said, pushing him away and straightening her bonnet. "You are worse than any child. Poor Mary will have hysterics."

But Mary, looking prettier and more animated than Alice had ever seen her, was giggling up at Piers and telling him again how silly he was. And he was laughing at both of them, his arm still about Mary. An elderly gentleman who was standing a short distance away with a lady was smiling with some amusement at them.

Alice turned sharply away and moved over to the cages of the birds. She had felt all her insides somersaulting. The old gentleman had undoubtedly seen them as a family. They must look like a family.

And Piers would be such a good father. He was

giving every appearance of enjoying the afternoon, not merely enduring the tedium of having to spend it in company with a child. He had made Mary forget all her peevishness and her aches and pains. The girl had become a child enjoying an outing.

He might have had a nine-year-old daughter now. Just two years younger than Mary. He might have been taking her about London and exerting himself to amuse her. And she might have had a ten-year-old son. Nicholas. She might have been showing him London. Instead they were both childless, both widowed, entertaining someone else's child.

She swallowed twice in quick succession.

"Did I offend you, Allie?" A hand squeezed her shoulder from behind. "I should not have grabbed you like that. It was not good for your dignity, was it? Forgive me, please. You know I am a careless fellow."

"No," she said, reaching up quickly and patting his fingers with her own. "It was not that, Piers. Quite the contrary. Mary is not your responsibility, and yet you have given up an afternoon to her amusement." She turned to look at her niece, who was still standing before the elephant's cage.

He bent down to look into her face, his hands clasped behind him. "Neither is she your responsibility," he said. "But she exists and is a child and has a right to some pleasure. And so we have given her pleasure. What is it, Allie?"

She smiled bleakly and shrugged. "Nothing," she said. "I just suddenly had the thought that you might have been here with your daughter or I with Nicholas. That is all. A flash of self-pity." She smiled more firmly.

"But we are not," he said gently. "We are here with your niece and each other. I'm sorry, Allie. Now, once every bird has been gazed at and remarked upon, I shall escort you both out to my curricle again and take you to Gunter's for ices." Mary had come up to them by that point. "That is, if you are good girls, of course. Only tea and cream cakes if you are not."

They were both judged worthy of ices a half hour later, though Mary announced when hers was half devoured that her mama would never allow her to have one for fear of drawing on a chill.

"It will have to be our secret, then," Piers said. "I won't tell if you don't, Mary. And we shall ask your aunt to raise her right hand and swear not to tell. Come along, Allie, let's see it."

She took the oath with great solemnity.

"But listen, Mary," he said gravely, "don't you dare catch a chill within the next month."

Mary giggled and promised.

"Now," he said, "shall we twist your aunt's arm and persuade her to join us at Astley's Amphitheater tomorrow afternoon?"

"Oh, yes, please!" Mary squealed. "Please, Aunt Alice. I daresay Papa will not let me go alone with Mr. Westhaven."

"I daresay he will not," Alice agreed. She looked at their grinning companion. "Are you quite sure, Piers? You must have a great many more important things to do."

He raised his eyebrows. "Not a single one," he said.

And so they spent another carefree afternoon together the next day, though they were forced to take Piers' closed carriage as rain threatened to fall.

Mary sat across from them on the return journey and lapsed into silence after having spent all of ten minutes reliving the equestrian wonders she had seen. She looked from one to the other of them.

"Are you going to marry Aunt Alice?" she asked Piers.

Alice wished fervently that it were possible to control one's blushes.

"No," he said at her side. "I don't believe your Aunt Alice would be very flattered at the idea, Mary."

"I don't see why not," Mary said. "Uncle Webster has been dead a very long time, and I would like to have you for an uncle."

"That is high praise indeed," he said. "I shall keep

it in mind. Now, I have not turned my head to look, but I will wager that your aunt's face is as crimson as the bow at your chin. Am I right?'' He turned a laughing face to Alice's.

''Mary,'' she said, knowing that the coolness of her voice was utterly belied by the color of her face. ''that is not the sort of thing you speak of in public, you know. It is not at all ladylike.''

''It is never considered genteel to put another lady to the blush,'' Piers said, amused eyes steady on Alice's face. ''Even when she looks very pretty doing it, Mary.''

Fortunately for Alice's peace of mind, he turned his head at that moment to wink at Mary.

Mr. Westhaven was pleased with the party he had arranged for Vauxhall. It should be quite easy to avoid the appearance of having committed himself irrevocably to Miss Borden. Since Vauxhall was an open-air pleasure garden attended by all and sundry, Mr. Bosley had agreed to be one of the party, which included also Lady Margam, Miss Borden, Alice, Sir Clayton Lansing (he had not intended to invite that particular gentleman, but had felt obliged to do so when Lansing had mentioned that Miss Borden had told him about it), Amanda and Jarvis Carpenter, Mr. King, and Miss Marks.

''I am vastly pleased that Bosley has agreed to be one of the party,'' he told Alice. ''You will like him, Allie.''

''Will I?'' she said. ''I must confess to a curiosity to converse with him, having heard so much about him.''

''You will find him genial and jovial,'' he said. ''And yet I swear, Allie, he would sell his grandmother if there were profit in it.''

''A delightful character,'' she said.

''One in a million,'' he said cheerfully.

She was to have her curiosity satisfied early in the evening, Alice discovered. Piers had decided that they would approach the gardens in the slow and cumbersome manner—by boat across the River Thames. It was also, of course, the most enchanting approach to Vauxhall. Mr. Bosley seated himself beside her in the boat, while Sir Clayton frowned and sat with Lady Margam. And he offered her his arm when they set foot on land again.

"If you do not consider it an impertinence for me to expect such a thing, Mrs. Penhallow," he said, "me being only in trade, you know, and some of the gentry considering that I must therefore have the plague." He laughed heartily at his own humor.

"Thank you, sir," she said. "I am very thankful for your arm."

"It is civil of you to say so, I am sure, ma'am," he said. "I have made something of a fortune for myself, it is true, but it is a notion of the gentry, I know, that they can be as poor as church mice, but it is still beneath their dignity to set their hands to some honest work. And how well set up was the late Mr. Penhallow, may I ask?"

Alice almost choked and turned an amused eye in Piers' direction. But his head was bent to hear something Amanda was saying.

"Thank you, sir," she said. "He left me with a competence."

"And his property went to . . . ?" He raised inquiring eyebrows.

"To his cousin, sir," she said.

"Ah, how sad for you," he said. "There were no children, ma'am?"

He patted her hand and clucked his tongue in sympathy. "But then you are young enough and lovely enough to attract yourself a handsome lord, if you choose," he said. "Or perhaps you will turn your eye next time to a man who can offer you a fortune and no titles." He laughed heartily.

Gracious, Alice thought, startled, was the man flirting with her? This time she did catch Piers' eye and he winked at her.

Mr. Bosley seated her beside him in the box Piers had reserved for the evening and even replaced her hand on his arm when he had taken his own chair.

"We will dance later, Mrs. Penhallow," he said genially, "when the orchestra strikes up with a country dance I know the steps to. I suppose you dance quadrilles and minuets and waltzes and all those. I do not. I hope you do not mind sitting for a while."

"Certainly not, sir," she said with some amusement. "The gardens and the lights are so enchanting."

"It is just to be hoped that those clouds do not bring rain until very much later," he said, "or even a storm. It has been hot enough today."

Alice murmured assent and sat back prepared to be entertained. Mr. Bosley told her all about his business and his many assets, for all the world as if he were making an offer to her papa, she thought.

"It is as well to let the young people frolic," he said affably after a few minutes when Piers was dancing with Miss Borden, Amanda with Mr. King, and Jarvis with Henrietta Marks. "It looks good to see young people happy together, does it not, Mrs. Penhallow?"

She thought how Piers would enjoy hearing his dancing described as frolicking and himself as one of the young people. But it did strike her suddenly that perhaps Mr. Bosley's interest in entertaining her was more a ruse to keep her away from Piers than a personal interest in her. Had he heard that they were friends? That they had spent some time together in the previous few weeks? Somehow the idea did not seem at all improbable now that she had met the man.

It was a suspicion that was further confirmed when Piers asked her to dance awhile later and Mr. Bosley immediately got to his feet and declared that she had promised the dance to him. It was a waltz.

She followed him to the dancing area with some amusement.

But it was not after all to be a thoroughly enjoyable

evening. The gardens were all she had ever dreamed they would be and more. The boxes were gaily decorated, the orchestra played lively music, the food was every bit as good as it was famed to be, and the colored lanterns gave a magical glow to the many trees and to the figures of the revelers below.

But her only escape from Mr. Bosley was with Sir Clayton, who led her onto the dance floor, also for a waltz, tried to hold her too close, and then suggested a walk along the lantern-lit paths. Before they returned to their box a half hour later, she had been forced to fend off yet another kiss and marriage proposal.

It was all very irritating, she thought, as they settled for supper. Yet when she tried to analyze the underlying causes of her irritation, she came up with two answers that only made her feel worse.

The weather was very close. There was not a breath of a breeze. There was a storm coming. She could feel it. It was giving her something of a headache. And the evening would be spoiled. The rain would probably come before the fireworks display. Hence her irritation.

The other cause was far more disturbing. She had had no private word with Piers all evening and had not danced with him even once. They were in surely the most enchanted spot in all of London, and the orchestra had played several waltzes. Yet not one of them had she danced with Piers. The fact irritated her.

And disturbed her a great deal when she had analyzed it. The sooner she returned to Bath, the sooner she could restore a measure of serenity to her mind.

# 9

---

IT was an evening Mr. Westhaven wished at an end even as he exerted himself to make sure all his guests were occupied and enjoying themselves. He had always enjoyed an evening at Vauxhall and was determined to make the most of this one. Having once set his mind on returning to the country, though, he found himself resenting every day that kept him from making the journey. He intended to set out the next day.

In the meanwhile Bosley seemed to have decided to make Allie the object of his gallantry. Piers was not at all surprised. She looked particularly fine in a dress of deep rose, her dark hair piled high, with curls at her neck and temples. And of course, she was far too well-bred to show any disgust at being singled out for attention by a mere cit. Indeed, he could see that she was amused by the situation, as he had known she would be. He had known Allie would appreciate Bosley's personality.

He danced with all his lady guests with the exception of Alice. She was being too jealously guarded by Bosley, and later was borne off by Lansing. He would have worried about her when the two of them disappeared along one of the paths, away from the dancing area. But he knew Alice had too much sense to consent to step off the main thoroughfare. He would wager, though, that Lansing would try to steal a kiss anyway.

By the time they all gathered in the box for supper, Piers was congratulating himself on the success of the evening and on his own success in singling out none of the ladies for marked attention. The only thing that threatened to spoil the evening—and he had no control over that—was the weather. It looked as if a storm might come up before the fireworks display. But he had had the carriages brought around over the bridge. They would not have far to run if the rain came down before they were ready to leave.

It was Mr. Bosley who suggested the walk. It would be a pleasant way to help their supper on its way down, he explained. But when Piers turned to claim Alice's company, it was to find her hand already resting on Bosley's portly arm. And even as he turned to Lady Margam, he found a little hand creeping beneath his arm and two large eyes peeping imploringly up at him for a brief moment.

"Miss Borden," he said, "would you care to walk with me?"

They all set out along the widest and most brightly lit path. The air was close and still, although a breeze was beginning to sway the upper branches.

"It will be raining within a half hour," Lady Margam said. "We had better not go too far."

"We will turn back as soon as the wind reaches us," Sir Clayton assured her.

"The trouble with ladies," Mr. Bosley said, "is that they are always afraid of having their hair blown about and of getting their dresses wet. There are plenty of places to shelter in the gardens."

"But not for an hour or more while a storm blows itself out, brother," Lady Margam said.

Mr. Bosley smiled genially down at Alice. "That depends entirely on the company one is in," he said.

Good Lord, Piers thought hilariously, Bosley really was flirting with Allie. He was going to have to watch to see that the man did not draw her down any of the less frequented paths. Perhaps she was going to have an offer of that fishy fortune after all. He pursed his lips and tried to catch her eye. But she was looking up to the treetops, her lips parted. She looked enchanted.

"I do beg your pardon," Cassandra was murmuring

at his side, "but I thought Sir Clayton was about to offer me his arm. I am afraid of him."

"Afraid?" he said. "Because the man has such good taste?"

"I am shy," she said. "I do not know what to talk about with other gentlemen. I feel comfortable with you. I do beg your pardon."

"I am honored to have your company," he said. "I am sorry. Am I walking too fast for you?"

"Just a little," she said apologetically. "I am wearing new slippers."

"Then we will stroll in a more leisurely fashion," he said, slowing his steps so that they fell to the back of the group.

The storm was going to come up far faster than they had anticipated, he noticed a mere few minutes later. The air grew chill, and the branches began to sway above their heads with loud, swishing sounds. The lanterns moved in the trees and the colored lights they cast swayed about, making even more of an enchanted land of the world below them. He must suggest that they turn back.

"Oh," Cassandra Borden said suddenly, "what was that?" She had stopped walking and was staring down one of the narrow, darkened paths to their left.

"What was what?" he asked. But even as he did so, she pulled her arm free of his and darted down the path.

What the devil? Piers stood still for a moment, not sure whether he should call ahead to the others to wait or pursue his companion before he lost her among the trees. It was a very dark path. He chose the latter course.

She stopped a short distance down the path and looked carefully about her. "Where did it go?" she asked.

"Where did what go?" He took her arm in a firm grasp.

"The kitten," she said. "A little lost, frightened kitten. Did you not see it?"

"No, I did not," he said. "It was doubtless a stray, Miss Borden. We had better return to the main path. I fear it is going to start raining soon. We should find the carriages without delay. The fireworks will have to wait until another night, I'm afraid."

"But we cannot abandon it," she said, sounding on the verge of tears. "Poor little lost kitten. I would not be able to sleep tonight for thinking of it out here, starving and alone."

Oh Lord, Piers thought, how did one explain to a sensitive young girl that looking for a kitten in Vauxhall Gardens was rather like looking for the proverbial needle in a haystack? And how did one explain that one did not wish to be alone with her for too long for fear of compromising her and putting oneself into an awkward position? He could imagine what some members of their party were already thinking about the fact that he had slunk down a darkened path with her.

"We must look farther," she said. "Just a little farther along, sir."

Well, perhaps twenty steps farther, he thought weakly, following her deeper into darkness.

"We must turn back now," he said gently a couple of minutes later. "Probably by this time the kitten has found its owner and is curled snugly on someone's lap." The trees were roaring above their heads.

"Oh," she said. She sounded on the verge of tears. "If only I could believe that were true. But we must do as you say. It is the only sensible thing to do."

She gazed about her one last time as she turned back toward him. But her arm stiffened in his, and she pointed eagerly along another path altogether.

"There it is," she said. "We are almost up to it, poor frightened little thing. Stay, kitty." And she advanced slowly along the path, one arm stretched out before her.

Piers addressed a speaking glance to the sky above their heads and followed her. That kitten must be a particularly senseless creature, he thought a minute or so later. It certainly seemed to have no interest in being taken to safety. Indeed, he had not himself glimpsed the animal and was beginning to have uncharitable thoughts about its very existence. If he did not know that Miss Borden was a timid young girl, he would be suspecting some trick.

She paused when they came within sight of one of the rustic shelters where people who could not afford one of the boxes, or people who wished to dine tête-à-tête, very often took their supper. But of the kitten there was still no sign.

"Oh," she said regretfully, turning back to him, "I am afraid we have lost him. He did not realize we had come to his rescue."

She was looking full up at him. He could see that in the sudden illumination of a flash of lightning. The next moment she was in his arms.

"Oh," she said, her voice panic-stricken, "there is a storm."

"It is not overhead yet," he said. "But we must hurry back."

Even as he spoke, a large drop of rain splashed onto his face, and the thunder rumbled in the distance.

"Oh, no," she said, clinging to him, "It is raining and the storm is close. We cannot go all that way in this. I am so frightened of storms."

"I will keep my arm about you," he said soothingly, "and we will move as fast as we can. You will be quite safe."

That was the moment when the heavens decided to open. He set an arm about her shoulders and rushed with her toward the shelter.

And there they were stuck, he thought, until the storm passed. Perhaps an hour, if he were lucky. Longer if he were not. Though length of time was really immaterial. However it turned out, he would be away from the group with Miss Borden for a considerable length of time. Indeed, it was probable that if the rest of them had turned back in time, they were already at the carriages and going home, leaving his carriage for his own and Miss Borden's use.

However he looked at it, the bottom line was the same. He was going to have to offer for the girl.

"Oh," she said, clinging to him and hiding her face against him as he seated them both on a bench that was away from the pelting rain. Another flash of lightning lit up the sky. "I am so very frightened. And so c-cold."

He unbuttoned his coat and drew her inside it with him. He wrapped his arms firmly about her and rocked her. He made soothing noises into her hair.

Devil take it!

And then somehow her face was raised to his, and he kissed her soft lips, very much as he would a frightened child. Except that she moaned and clung to him, and he was forced to deepen the kiss.

"I feel safe here with you," she said several minutes later, curled up on his lap where he had lifted her, her head burrowed into the warm spot between his neck and shoulder.

"You *are* safe," he said soothingly. "I have you safe."

The thunder crashed around them.

Had that kitten existed? he wondered.

So he was holding his future bride. Very soft and warm and shapely. A soft, eager mouth that had offered to open for him if he had accepted the invitation. A tender heart. The mother of his children. Except that for all the shapeliness and warm eagerness, he could not picture himself making love to the girl. She was a child herself. Too young to have children of her own. They would probably kill her.

He would end up killing her, as he had killed Harriet. And loving her just as little.

He held her close against him and rocked her soothingly. And he stared unseeingly into the darkness, which was lit every few seconds by lightning.

He wondered what Alice was doing.

Alice and the others had turned back almost as soon as Cassandra and Piers had left the main path. The

absence of the one couple was noted immediately, and
Lady Margam was instantly worried, but Mr. Bosley
just laughed in his genial way and said that the naughty
puss had merely stepped off the path for a minute at
the insistence of her beau and would be back with
them before they knew it.

"This is certainly the place for young love to thrive,
do you not agree, Mrs. Penhallow?" he said.

But when they returned to the box and there was
still no sign of the missing couple either there or coming up behind them, Mr. Bosley insisted that they
hurry to the carriages without further delay, as most
other people were doing.

"Doubtless they have gone straight there instead of
coming here first," he said, taking Alice's arm within
his again.

But the truants were not at the carriages, either, and
the rain was beginning to fall. There had been one
flash of lightning and its following rumble of thunder
already.

"You must go and look for them, brother," Lady
Margam said.

But Mr. Bosley shouted with laughter. "I could
search for hours, Lucinda," he said, "and then not be
thanked when I came up to them." He shook his head.
"Young love! I shall have something to say to young
Cassie tomorrow, you may be bound, and to Mr.
Westhaven, too. Forcing my hand in this way! It is
almost enough to put me out of humor."

Except that he did not look at all out of humor,
Alice thought. She was sick with worry. Somehow,
she was sure, that girl had contrived to draw Piers
away and keep him away. And now, unless they appeared immediately—and even perhaps then—the girl
would be hopelessly compromised and Piers trapped
into a marriage he had decided he did not want.

He was to return to Westhaven Park the next day.

"You will come in my carriage, if you will,
ma'am," Mr. King was saying to her as the rain began

to come down in earnest. "I have Miss Carpenter and her brother with me, too."

"It would by my pleasure, ma'am," Mr. Bosley said one moment later, but Alice climbed quickly into Mr. King's carriage out of the rain.

"Bosley will convey Miss Marks and Lansing home," Mr. King was explaining to Jarvis. "Westhaven's carriage will be left for his and Miss Borden's use."

Alice did not notice the grin Jarvis and Mr. King exchanged. She was peering anxiously through the window. But there was no sign of either Piers or Cassandra Borden as the carriages drew away.

Piers dismissed his carriage before it reached St. James's Street. The roads and pavements were still very wet and the air chilly and damp, though the rain had stopped some time before and there were even some stars in the sky. It would have been far more comfortable to ride, he supposed, but he could not do it. He could not go home and to bed.

Where would he go instead? To one of his clubs? But he did not feel like making conversation or playing cards or getting drunk. For the moment all he felt like doing was walking. And if some footpad decided that he was a likely target for attack, then God help the poor man. He would be delighted to tear him limb from limb.

He had taken Miss Borden home once the storm had eased—more than an hour after they had taken refuge in the shelter at Vauxhall Gardens. Her mother had taken her tearfully into her arms. Bosley had greeted him like a long-lost son, with smiles and joviality, and offered him a glass of something to warm him.

But he had declined and excused himself after assuring the uncle that he would return in the morning, if he might.

*If* he might! Doubtless the whole of the fishy fortune would be put to use to hire professional murderers if he failed to put in an appearance and make his offer.

And now he was getting his just deserts for all the amusement he had derived from Bosley's character. The more he thought of it, the more he was convinced that somehow Bosley had put Miss Borden up to luring him away as she had, just before the storm broke. The timing had been quite perfect.

It must have been Bosley. Miss Borden would never have thought of that for herself. He felt angry with the man. How could he have taken such a risk with his niece's virtue in order to net a husband for her? What if his victim had turned out to be an unscrupulous man? He could, if he wished, have enjoyed the girl for more than an hour there at the gardens, without much fear of interruption. Such was her innocence, he did not believe she would have even put up any resistance.

Well, he was done for now. Leg-shackled. A tenant-for-life. All the rest of the clichés. And perhaps it was just as well. He had cheerfully agreed only a few weeks before that it was time he married again and added a few hopeful infants to the human race. It had seemed the right thing to do. His mother would be pleased. And he supposed that he could not do much better than Cassandra Borden. She was very young and very pretty and doubtless biddable.

He might as well do the thing quickly. Make his offer the next day. Marry the girl before the end of the Season. Doubtless Bosley would think nothing but St. George's with half the *ton* in attendance to be good enough for his niece. He could take her into the country even before the Season was quite over, and live at Westhaven for as long as he wished.

By this time next year he would probably be a father. He would like that, at least. Yes, he would like that.

Provided he did not kill her in the process. His footsteps increased in pace.

Perhaps he would take her to meet his mother tomorrow afternoon. Mama would like her, as she had liked Harriet. Another family member to bully. Poor Miss Borden. He would have to be sure to sit next to her to give her the support she would need to see her through the meeting.

And where the deuce was he going? He stopped walking and looked about him, frowning. What the devil was he doing on Cavendish Square? And what time was it? He looked about him almost as if he expected to see the sun rising over the eastern horizon. It must be all of midnight.

Allie. Was that where he was going? As usual? Feel depressed, feel troubled about something, and run to Web and Allie. They would make him feel better.

Piers strolled onward in self-disgust until he stopped before the Penhallow house. Without even realizing it, he had come running to her. Poor Allie. She was doubtless disgusted by his disappearance at Vauxhall. She would be less than thankful to have him unburden all his woes on her shoulders at this hour of the night.

He was going to have to learn to live without her. He had become far too dependent on their friendship over the years. It had been all right, he supposed, while Web was still alive. But not now. There would be all sorts of people who would misunderstand their relationship. A close friendship between a man and a woman was too suspect a relationship to many people. Especially now that he was to take a bride again.

Bosley had seen it already. He had made every effort to keep him and Allie apart that evening.

Piers stood on the pavement, looking up to the lighted windows of Alice's private apartments, and fought the temptation to climb the steps and knock on the door.

Alice had dismissed her maid for the night. She had undressed and brushed out her hair. But she was not ready for bed yet. She would not be able to sleep. She put on a robe over her nightgown and took a book into her sitting room.

But she could not concentrate on that, either, she realized after more than five minutes had passed and she had not turned a single page. She closed the book and tossed it onto a table with some impatience.

She had her own life to lead. And now it was her own again, now that Phoebe was past the stage of even being able to pretend to weakness. She was free again. She certainly did not need to take anyone else's burdens on her shoulders.

Certainly not Piers'. He was a man of mature years, perfectly capable of organizing and living his own life. Except that there had always been a vulnerability about Piers, a strange innocence despite the detached, ironic view of the world he liked to take. He had been led into a trap, and he probably did not even know it.

He would have no choice but to marry the girl. Alice had thought of all the possible ways out of the situation that he might have, but there were none. Somehow the girl had trapped him alone with her in Vauxhall Gardens for the duration of the storm. There were several people who knew about it. Piers would have no choice.

And she did not believe that Mr. Bosley would allow him to forget it. She shuddered a little. Piers had always seemed so amused by Mr. Bosley, and she had been inclined to share that amusement at the start of the evening. She no longer did so.

Piers had been picked out from the start as an eligible husband for Cassandra Borden, and he had not had a chance from that moment on. Mr. Bosley and Miss Borden were a pair of connivers worthy of each other. She did not know which was the more responsible for what had happened that evening, but she did not doubt that both were quite ready to make the most of its success.

Poor Piers. He probably did not even suspect that he had been had. And he had been so close to doing what he really wanted to do and really ought to do—going back to Westhaven Park.

Alice got to her feet and paced the sitting room restlessly. She must shake it from her mind. Piers was her friend. That was all. There was no other tie that bound them. He was not her concern. And since there was nothing she could do to extract him from the predicament in which he found himself, there was no point in giving herself a sleepless night over it.

She must go to bed. She needed to be fresh in the morning. She was to begin her own journey home during the afternoon. Home. Bath. She longed for it and dreaded it. Longed for the peace and predictability of her life there. Dreaded putting behind her the life and excitement that the past few weeks had brought her. The Tower. Astley's. The visit to Lady Neyland. Somerset House. The Egyptian Hall. Piers.

Piers. Perhaps she would never see him again. And she was not sure that she would want to see him once he was married to Cassandra Borden. The girl would lead him a merry dance, she feared. Not that it was any of her concern. It was not her concern at all. She must go to bed and put it from her.

She wandered restlessly to the window and put back one curtain so that she could gaze down upon the square. It was lit up by moonlight now, the only sign of the storm the puddles of water on the street. How the storm had played into the girl's hands!

There was a man standing in the street below. Alice took a hasty step back and let the curtain fall over the window again. But she recognized him even as she did so, and she stepped forward once more and lifted the curtain.

It was Piers. He raised a hand in greeting as she gazed down at him.

She hesitated for only a moment before picking up a candle from the mantel and running quietly down the stairs and across the hallway to slide the bolts back from the door. Her heart pounded and she bit down on her lower lip, feeling for all the world like an escaping prisoner afraid of waking the guards.

But the bolts slid back without noise, and she pulled the door open.

# 10
---

PIERS climbed the stairs behind Alice.

"You don't have to say it," he said. "I know I have no business being here, Allie. It must be fiendishly late, is it? You ought not to have looked out through the window, you know. I had no intention of knocking at the door."

She set the candle down and turned to look at him. "You walked all this way," she said, "in order to look at the house? At least, I assume you walked."

"I was not thinking at all of where I was going," he said. "When I came to myself, here I was. But I would have moved on again in another moment. Don't scold, Allie, please." He slumped down into a chair.

"I am not scolding you," she said. "Oh, Piers, I suppose you have been wandering around in that damp coat. You will catch a chill."

"Is it damp?" He brushed his shoulder in some surprise. "So it is. I suppose I should take it off before it dampens your furniture. Do you mind, Allie?"

She smiled fleetingly. "Your being here at all is so horrifyingly improper," she said, "that I suppose one more small impropriety will be scarcely noticed, Piers. Take it off, do."

He stood up to shrug out of the garment. He hung it over the back of another chair. "I'm glad you are not one of those females who have a fit of the vapors at the very thought of a man in his shirtsleeves," he said with a grin. "I haven't seen you with your hair down since you were a girl, Allie, and then you usually had it in two braids." His eyes moved down to her night robe, and he pursed his lips briefly before sitting down again.

"Well," he said, "how did you enjoy the evening? Vastly entertaining, was it not?"

"No," she said quietly, seating herself on the love seat.

"What?" he said. "You did not appreciate Bosley's conversation, Allie? He did not tell you all about the fishy fortune? He did not hint that perhaps he might lavish some of it on you? I could have sworn that he was flirting with you. Or perhaps paying serious court."

"I do not particularly like him," she said.

He raised his eyebrows. "Too vulgar for you, Allie?" he said. "I am surprised. I thought you would have been amused."

"No," she said.

"I had a wonderful time," he said. "The storm could not have come at a more opportune moment. I had the great felicity of spending upward of an hour in a sylvan grotto with the delectable Miss Borden."

"And I suppose," she said quietly, "that she was terrified of storms."

"Ah," he said, "how did you know? She clung beautifully. I had to take her right onto my lap. And the best comfort I could offer seemed to be kisses. What more could any gentleman ask of an evening, Allie?"

She looked steadily at his smiling face. "Piers," she said.

"You disapprove?" he said. "You think it immoral to kiss a female before marriage? You are being overly prim, Allie. Old-fashioned."

"Piers," she said. "Don't."

He grinned at her. "But what is a gentleman to do," he asked, "when a young female offers her lips so sweetly? And lips trembling with fright at that? He would have to be made of marble to resist the invitation. Besides, it would be ungentlemanly, would it not?"

She looked down at her hands in her lap.

"The marriage will follow, of course," he said. "You did not think I would spend an hour kissing an innocent young girl and then refuse to do the honorable thing, did you, Allie? I am not quite such an unprincipled fellow, you know. Come, wish me joy."

"Oh, Piers," she said. "An _innocent_ young girl?"

"Well, of course," he said. "A few kisses from a lecherous, careless fellow have not destroyed her innocence, Allie. She needed comforting. She had no idea of the peril she was in, coming onto my lap as she did and offering her lips. No idea at all. She is all trust and innocence."

Alice said nothing.

"Westhaven Park will doubtless be filled with children within the next few years," he said. "Baron Berringer will be able to decline into old age, confident of the fact that the succession is assured for a long time to come. Bosley will have a home for his fishy fortune. And Mama will have her grandchildren. Come now, you must admit that it has been a vastly profitable evening. You cannot be so poor-spirited as not to wish me joy, Allie."

"No," she said, "I can't. I want you to be happy, Piers. I want it so very much. I hope you will be happy with Miss Borden. I do hope so."

"I _do_ hope you will not mind being executed," he said in imitation of the tone she had used. "I _do_ hope you will not mind having a noose around your neck. I _do_ hope not." He grinned at her.

"No," she said, smiling back. "I meant what I said, Piers. I know you will make the best of it. I know you will be a good husband. And father."

He sat back in his chair suddenly, put back his head, and closed his eyes. His hands lightly gripped the arms of the chair.

"I should not have come here," he said, "and I should be going now. Shouldn't I? Tell me to leave, Allie."

"Why did you come?" she asked. "What do you need?"

He turned his head on the cushion and smiled at her. "Ointment and bandages," he said, "and painkillers. And a cool hand and soothing words."

She merely looked at him.

"Peace," he said, "and comfort and safety. Everything I have always found with you, Allie. And with Web, of course. Do you think I might stay here for the rest of my life?" He grinned.

"But I have no comfort to offer," she said. "I wish I did, Piers."

He laughed softly. "Ah, but you don't have to say any words," he said. "You only have to *be,* Allie. I have never known anyone else whose very presence can exude an aura of peace and home. At Chandlos. In this house. Particularly in this room. I think I could be placed blindfold in this room and know it was yours. How do you do it?"

She smiled uncertainly at him, and he closed his eyes again. But he sighed after a couple of moments and opened them once more.

"What a selfish wretch I am!" he said. "Keeping you from your bed at well after midnight and almost falling asleep in your sitting room, all because I need comfort and reassurance. You should have kicked me out long ago, Allie. But I am going. And it is good-bye for a while, is it not? You are returning to Bath tomorrow?"

"Yes," she said.

He got up from his chair, took her by the hands, and drew her to her feet.

"I am going to miss you," he said, raising first one hand and then the other to his lips. "God, how I will miss you, Allie."

"And I you," she said.

"Doubtless it will be a relief to be free of me and my troubles," he said with a flashing grin. "What, Allie? Tears? Oh, come now. I have done nothing to be worthy of your tears, have I?"

She shrugged and swallowed.

His hands tightened on hers. "It is always hard to

say good-bye, is it not?'' he said, leaning forward to kiss her on the cheek.

''Yes,'' she said, ''always hard. Good-bye, then, Piers.'' She smiled at him through her tears. And she stretched up to kiss him softly on the cheek.

But it was almost impossible for him to make the move to drop his hold of her hands, pick up his coat, and turn to the door. Hard to know that tomorrow she would not be here. Or the next. Or the next.

And she did not have the willpower to remove her hands from his, smile more firmly, and say something commonplace that would send him on his way. She did not have the willpower to send him through that door, knowing that he might never come through it again, or through any of the doors into her life.

''Allie,'' he said, and bent his head and kissed her briefly, softly on the lips. He looked questioningly, anxiously into her eyes.

But she could not see him. And she fought for control, biting her upper lip, gripping his hands more tightly until finally—gratefully—his hands released hers to come about her and draw her against him, and she could put her own up about his neck and hide her face in the folds of his neckcloth.

''Allie,'' he said again against her ear, his voice low. And one hand was twining in her hair and one thumb was stroking over her cheek and ear, and she gave up the struggle. She gave up everything. Nothing mattered any longer except this moment. She raised her head and sought his mouth.

He was home. At last. After thirty-six years. Everything in his life, everything in his soul, was in his arms and he would think of nothing except the world and the universe that he held to himself. There was the soft silkiness of her dark hair and its enticing fragrance. And the cool silk of her robe and the warm, slim woman's body beneath it. And then there was her mouth open to his, eager, clinging, tasting of the salt of her tears.

Allie. Allie.

She kept her eyes firmly closed when his mouth moved to her throat and one shoulder. She felt the rippling muscles of his shoulders with searching palms and felt his firm male body with her breasts and her stomach and her thighs. She arched herself to him, wanting him with an ache that throbbed in her.

Piers!

And then his mouth was back on hers, his tongue probing, teasing, stroking.

"Allie."

The one word, whispered. The one question. He looked down into a face that was beautiful for him, lips swollen, cheeks flushed, eyes heavy with passion. And he gazed into her face, his own asking the question, searching for the answer in her eyes, in her mouth. Allie?

And she gazed upward into the face of all her dreams. Not just Piers' face, though that too. Oh, yes, that too. But the face of her dream. Piers wanting her and loving her. Focused entirely on her. Asking her the question with the one whispered word and with eyes that pleaded and were not quite sure of her answer.

She reached up to touch his cheek with trembling fingertips and swallowed awkwardly. And answered his question. He stopped to take her up in his arms, and she closed her eyes and rested her head on his shoulder.

He opened the door that he supposed must lead to her dressing room. The door opposite it, the one leading to her bedchamber, was open. The bedclothes had been turned down for the night. A single candle burned on a side table.

His hands were on the ribbon at her throat and untying it. And untying the ribbon at her waist. And pushing the silk from her shoulders and down her arms. She lay quietly, looking up at him. And she was lost no longer. She was lying on her bed in Cavendish Square and Piers was sitting on the edge of it in his shirtsleeves, undressing her. Her nightgown was following the robe, being drawn down over her body. She had never been naked with a man.

He was worshiping her with his eyes. He was going to make love to her. She reached up to loosen the folds of his neckcloth, to undo the buttons of his shirt. And his mouth came down lightly on hers and his hands twined in her hair as her own worked.

He did not extinguish the candle when he joined her on the bed. He wanted to see her. He wanted to watch her eyes as he loved her. And he loved her slowly—with his hands and with his mouth, wanting her and wanting her, not wanting this loving ever to end. And she loved him in return, her hands on him an agony of sweetness and heat. He watched her eyes wanting him, knowing him, loving him.

She wanted it to last forever. She wanted him in her. She wanted release. She could not endure much longer without release. But not yet. Not yet. She wanted the wanting him to go on forever. She did not want thought or sanity or the cold and cruel world to come back. She wanted this to go on forever.

"Allie," he said against her mouth. "My beautiful Allie."

"Love me," she whispered. "Go on loving me, Piers. Don't stop."

Never, he promised her with his eyes.

He would never stop loving her. Never. But this loving. Oh, this loving. He needed her. He needed her now.

She looked back into his eyes as he positioned her for the final loving, and spread her hands palm up on either side of her head for his own to cover. And she looked into his eyes as he came into her, biting only momentarily on her lower lip as he began to move in her.

And he watched her, a woman in the act of love. *His* woman. His world. But she was too beautiful. Too desirable. Too warm and inviting around his pain. He could no longer prolong the sweet agony. He buried his face in her hair and pressed his palms against her own as he drove his desire and his love into her until everything, the whole universe, shattered against his closed eyelids. And yet it was not a lone experience, even though he had not been able to continue to look into her eyes. She shuddered beneath him at the identical moment, and their fingers twined together.

She continued to tremble beneath the full force of his relaxed weight as her whole body sought to adjust to the release that had begun there, where he had loved her. But body and mind knew alike that he was Piers, that she had given all of herself to him, with nothing held back. She knew it, and she reveled in the knowledge. For all her life she would know that they had been lovers for one brief and glorious night.

When he moved to her side and pulled the bedclothes up around them, she lifted her head obediently so that his arm could come about her and relaxed down against it. She looked fully into his eyes. She smiled and tilted her face for his warm and lingering kiss. And then she smiled at him again.

He smiled back and marveled at how the events of less than an hour could remove from his eyes the scales that he had placed there quite deliberately and forgotten about years before. He marveled at how he could finally see again, and at how bright and colorful the world was to eyes that were not blind.

He gazed silently into her eyes and into her smiling face until she finally closed her eyes and fell asleep. And he continued to watch her, sleep being the furthest need from his mind.

For now that passion was sated, reality was returning. Had returned. He held in his arms, her warm and naked body against his own, the woman he had fallen in love with fourteen years before when she was a graceful girl newly become a woman. He had thought of nothing but his infatuation for several weeks, wondering how both she and her father, the rector, would welcome the suit of a fellow who had run wild through his youth and early manhood and had nothing to recommend him except his name and his wealth and his property—none of which would have weighed more than a feather with either of the two people he would wish to impress.

He had paid dearly for his secrecy, for his lack of courage in coming to the point. For if he had had little enough chance of winning her anyway, he had had none at all after Web had confided his love for her and his determination to marry her. He had been quite unable to compete against Web. Not just because Web had everything to offer while he had nothing, but because Web was dearer to him than a brother. And he would not allow a woman to come between them. Especially a woman who deserved Web a thousand times more than she deserved him.

And so he had lost her before he had ever had a chance of having her. And had determinedly, over the next several years, pushed the pain and the longing into the background of his mind, forced friendship to the fore, and won his battle. He had made her into his dearest friend—along with Web. Always, safely, with Web, their names linked inextricably in his mind. Never Allie. Never once Allie until after Web's death. Always Web-and-Allie.

And now Allie again. For the last two years. Keeping himself away from Westhaven Park while she was still at Chandlos, making every excuse for doing so except the real one. And not wanting to return to Westhaven ever again once she moved away to Bath, but wanting and wanting to go there to see her. For friendship's sake. Merely because she was his dearest friend. His only dearest friend now that she was alone.

And now, since her arrival in London, the need to see her daily, the excuses to see her, the brightness of his days, knowing that in so many hours he would see her again, be with her again. Because she was his friend. Only because she was his friend. What other reason could there be?

He smiled rather bitterly up into the near darkness.

The candle, he realized suddenly, had gone out. God, the light had gone out. He was in darkness.

Allie. The woman he had loved in different ways for fourteen years. But always deeply. Always more deeply than he had loved anyone or anything else, including himself. Especially himself. Indeed, he was very close to hating himself at that moment.

What had he done?

He had come to her in his need, forced himself into her private apartments at midnight or later, forced her to listen to his woes while he calmed himself with her presence. He had forced her to wish him well in his coming marriage, and then he had been incapable of taking his leave of her.

Tomorrow she would have been free of him. She would have been on her way back to the life she had chosen for herself. And he had been unable to let her go.

He had played on her sympathy for him, her friendship, her willingness always to listen to him and comfort him. And he had violated her. He had forced her into something for which she would hate herself the next day, when she had finally realized what she had done.

God, he had slept with Web's wife. He closed his eyes, appalled at the realization. And she had given herself to him, not just from sympathy but with more passion than he had ever known in a woman. Allie. Who had been without Web for two years. He had come to her after midnight in her own rooms. At a time when she had been at her most vulnerable.

He hated himself with a depth of hatred he had never felt for anyone else.

He could not marry her. For several reasons he could not marry her. He had compromised another lady that night—oh, yes, another young innocent—and was duty bound to offer for her the next day. And he had known that full well when he had reached out for Allie. It was Cassandra Borden he must marry, not Allie.

And even if it were not so, even if he were as free

as he had been that morning, he could not marry Allie. How could he doom her to spend the rest of her days with him? When she had known Web? When she was Allie? How could he take advantage of the need he had so carelessly and selfishly aroused in her? How could he marry her when he knew that she would spend every day of her life pining for his friend?

And yet he had made love to her. And in the process killed everything. Killed the one good thing in his life. For they could no longer be friends. From tomorrow on they would find it almost impossible to look at each other. They would never be able to do so without remembering what had happened between them on this particular night. She would hate him. And he would hate himself, knowing that.

And so this was the end. The end of a friendship that had brightened his life through most of his adulthood. Not the end of his love. Now that he was conscious of it again, that would live on, perhaps for the rest of his life. But not as a light and a warmth. It would become dark and bitter, the knowledge that his love had been a selfish thing, reaching for its own gratification and destroying the peace of his beloved.

For Allie would suffer for what she had done this night. And he would be the last person on this earth who could comfort her.

She stirred at his side and opened her eyes. In the semidarkness he watched her look of bewilderment fade almost instantly. She smiled at him, and he bent his head and kissed her mouth. And continued to do so, warmly, lightly, so that he would not have to speak to her.

"Mm," she said sleepily, and her arm came about his chest.

He hated his own weakness, his vulnerability. At least the first time he had taken himself by surprise, he had acted from instinct, thought having played very little part in what had happened. He had no such excuse this time. He knew what he did and what needs in her he played upon. And he knew that tomorrow their friendship would be at an end and he would go off to make his offer to another woman. He knew his own selfishness, his own evil.

He turned her on the bed and came into her without foreplay. And he spent a long, long time moving in her, taking her slowly through the stages of arousal, and gradually—very gradually—to climax, drawing a cry of abandonment and pleasure from her at the end. And kissing her and holding her with a desperate tenderness and self-loathing when it was all over again.

He got out of bed and dressed himself in the darkness. And he bent over her and spoke the first coherent words he had said to her since their first lovemaking had begun.

"Don't get up," he said. "I will see myself out."

But of course she had to come downstairs with him in order to bolt the door again, so that the servants would not know that anyone had been there. She put on her nightgown and robe again.

He took her into his arms when they were downstairs and held her close, rocking her against him.

"Allie," he said against her hair, "forgive me if you ever can."

He saw only the beginnings of her calm smile before letting himself out through the door and closing it behind him again without looking back.

Alice went back upstairs, dropped her robe beside the bed, and lay down again—on the side of the bed where Piers had lain, on her stomach, her nose buried in the pillow.

She would not think before morning. She would not allow herself to think. She would only feel. There was the soreness left by his lovemaking—the delicious soreness that was almost a throbbing. And there was the languor from that second, lengthy encounter finished only a few minutes before and still leaving its weakness and its drowsiness.

And there was all the wonder of a fifteen-year-old

love now come to a glorious consummation. She would glory in the wonder of it.

She would not think. She would not recognize until the next day that what Piers had been saying downstairs was good-bye. She would let that fact reach her consciousness tomorrow.

But despite all, despite the pain and the wretchedness that she knew were ahead for her, she would not permit herself to regret what had just happened.

Never that.

She was living through the most wonderful night of her life. And there was still some of it left. There was still the warmth and the smell of him in her bed, and there were still all the effects of his lovemaking on her body to be enjoyed.

She must never allow herself to feel either regret or remorse.

# 11

MR. WESTHAVEN was clearly expected when he arrived in Russell Square late the following morning. Cassandra was nowhere in sight, as was proper. Mr. Bosley and Lady Margam were in the lower salon, looking rather as if they were awaiting a call from royalty, Piers thought.

Lady Margam was inclined to be tearful and worried that her daughter was far too young to be considering matrimony. Though if she must marry, of course, the mother could think of no one more suitable than Margam's dear friend.

Piers clasped his hands behind him and bowed in acknowledgment of the compliment.

Mr. Bosley was jovial and shook his guest heartily by the hand. He had seen young love at work the evening before, and who was he to stand in its way? Though of course, his little Cassie might have aspired to the hand of a duke if she had not fallen in love with a mere mister determined to turn her head.

He chuckled merrily as he shook Mr. Westhaven by the hand again.

Piers smiled and made a suitable reply. He was invited to take a seat.

What was she doing now? Was she up yet? Yes, of course she would be up. It was not Allie's way to lie in bed until noon. And probably she had not slept anyway, any more than he had. Was she getting ready for her journey to Bath? Had she left already?

Mr. Bosley became businesslike. He was prepared to settle such and such a dowry on Cassie's husband the day after the wedding—"for there is more to making a marriage than merely speaking a few words at the altar, as you will know, my dear sir." He named a sum that had Piers raising his eyebrows in surprise.

Mr. Bosley waved a hand at Mr. Westhaven's protestations that he had no need of such a dowry, that he was well able to support a wife and a family, too. Perhaps it would be better to put the money in trust for Miss Borden and any children of the marriage.

But that would not do, either. Much as Mr. Bosley was fond of his niece, he would not give tuppence for the female brain, especially when it came to managing money.

"No, my dear sir," he said magnanimously, "the money will be yours the morning after the night before, so to speak, to do with as you wish. If you are foolish enough to settle it on Cassie, then so be it. A man in love has been known to do worse things, I suppose." Another hearty laugh.

How was she feeling this morning? Wretched with remorse and guilt? He need not phrase it in his mind as a question. He had been trying all night and all morning not to think of how she must be feeling. But he had not been able to go to her. That was no longer an option in his life.

Mr. Bosley would have the contract all ready to sign a week later. "Not that I could not have had it ready this morning, sir," he explained. "But it is as well in such matters not to rush. And we know, of course, that your word as a gentleman is every bit as valuable as your signature on a contract."

Piers inclined his head again at the compliment.

But should he at least have called on her this morning to explain to her that it had all been his fault, that she must not blame herself at all? Should he have gone at least to apologize to her? But how was an apology possible? "I am sorry that I burst in upon you last night and violated you?" It was impossible. It was better far to stay away. He would be the very last person she would want to see during the rest of her lifetime.

"Ma'am." He turned to Lady Margam. "With your leave, may I have a few minutes alone with your daughter? Or under your chaperonage, if you prefer."

She rose to her feet. "I trust you with Cassandra, Mr. Westhaven," she said. "I shall send her down to you here. Brother?"

Mr. Bosley crossed the room to her and set a hand on the door handle. "Ho," he said, "Cass has probably paced a mile in her room this morning. And doubtless slept not a wink last night. I'll wager you did not either, sir." He chuckled at his own joke and opened the door for his sister to precede him into the hallway.

But perhaps he should have called anyway. How can one step out of a woman's bed and out of her life? He had done it before on numerous occasions, of course. But this was entirely different. A thousand, a million times different. How could he just walk out on Allie as if she were a whore not worth revisiting?

He shuddered. She would not, of course, put that interpretation on his absence.

It was strange, he thought a few minutes later, how sight had been restored to him the night before and had taken away more than one form of blindness. For this morning Miss Borden's timidity, her inability even to peep up at him from beneath her lashes, appeared totally false. She had been in company with him frequently in the past few weeks. The evening before, she had taken refuge from the storm on his lap and in his arms. And yet this morning she could not look at him.

But would he be able to raise his eyes to Allie this morning?

"I have spoken with your mother and your uncle this morning," he told the girl's bowed head. "They have both approved my suit. Your mother has permitted me to have a few minutes of your time so that I might have the honor of asking you to be my wife. Will you, Miss Borden?''

''Oh,'' was all she said, and pleated the skirt of her muslin dress between her fingers.

She wanted more. Well, then, he thought. ''I have grown fond of you in the past few weeks,'' he said. ''I can think of no greater joy than making you my wife.''

Allie. Where was she now? What was she doing?

''It is not because of last evening?'' the girl asked. She peeped up at him briefly then. ''Not because I chased after that poor little kitten and you were forced to shelter from the storm with me? Mama scolded me roundly for such an indiscretion.''

He stepped forward and took one of her hands. ''No, of course it is not because of that,'' he lied. ''You must have known before that that I had a partiality for you.''

''Oh,'' she said. ''It is just that I have always been determined, you see, to marry someone I loved. Uncle wants me to marry you because you are rich and are to be Lord Berringer one day. But that does not matter to me. I care to marry only a gentleman who loves me.''

Allie. Allie.

''Well, then,'' he said, raising her hand to his lips, ''I can see no bar to our marriage at all, Miss Borden, unless you do not love me.''

She raised her eyes full to his. Large, innocent eyes. Except that his own eyes were no longer blind. She wanted his very soul, it seemed. Well, she would have it. He had no more use for it himself.

''For of course I love you,'' he said, kissing her hand again.

''Oh,'' she said, making a little rosebud of her mouth and continuing to gaze, rapt, into his eyes.

He bent his head and kissed her. And kept his lips on hers when her own pressed sweetly against them.

He smiled at her. ''And will you keep me in suspense?'' he asked. ''Am I to be accepted or rejected?''

''Oh, I will marry you, sir,'' she said and blushed prettily.

''Splendid!'' he said. ''We shall make the wedding soon, shall we, so that we may remove to Westhaven Park for the summer?''

''Oh,'' she said, ''I do not think we should waste the rest of the Season, sir, when Mama has gone to so much trouble to bring me here and when Uncle has spent so much money on ball gowns and all the rest. And I have heard that Brighton is lovely in the summer.''

''Have you?'' he said. ''I believe your mama will disapprove of my being alone with you any longer, Miss Borden. Perhaps we can discuss our future plans at another time. Would you care to call on my mother with me this afternoon?''

''Oh,'' she said, ''on such a lovely day, sir? It would be a pity to sit indoors when the sun is shining. I would far prefer to drive in the park.''

''Then the park it will be,'' he said, bowing.

He wished, ten minutes later, as he drove away in his curricle, that he had brought a horse instead. He would have taken it into Hyde Park and galloped until its legs collapsed under it. On second thought, perhaps it was as well that he had not ridden. He had never been one for cruelty to animals.

So, he was an engaged man. Engaged to marry a very young girl who had learned somehow during her eighteen years how to get exactly what she wanted out of life. A girl who had picked her man and won him over the course of a few weeks despite his own reluctance. A girl who now intended to use her new status and his wealth to enjoy all that life in high society could offer.

A girl he did not love and now feared that he could not even like. A girl with whom he was going to have to take a very firm hand from his wedding day on if he did not wish to be ruled for the rest of his life. She was to be his wife, mistress of Westhaven Park, mother of his children. She was to be his life's companion.

He slowed his curricle when a carter he narrowly missed scowled at him and a round lady tending a vegetable stall shook her fist and favored him with the full extent of her profane vocabulary.

He dined at White's in splendid isolation, owing to the scowls he directed at anyone who looked as if he might be approaching. And he walked afterward for miles, he knew not where. It was two o'clock when he arrived in Cavendish Square again. But this time he did not stand outside, gazing up at the windows. He knocked on the door.

But of course, it was as he had fully expected it to be. She had left an hour before, her servant told him. And now belatedly, as he walked away, he realized that he should have called on her that morning even before going to Bosley's. He had owed her a call, awkward and painful as it would have been to both of them.

But he had forced her to get through the morning somehow alone. He had forced her to leave without a word of apology, without a word to assure her that what had happened had not been intentional seduction, that he respected her still, more than any other woman he knew, that it had all been his fault.

Or was it as well that cowardice had kept him away? Was it self-indulgence—yet again—to wish that he had seen her just one more time? Was it better for her that he had failed to put even more turmoil into her morning than there must already have been?

It was time to walk home and change and get himself ready to take his betrothed driving in the park.


Alice rose early, even earlier than usual, though she had slept deeply through the night. She had several things to do before setting out on the journey home after luncheon. She had last-minute instructions to give to the servants who would remain in London and to her maid, who would accompany her. She had some shopping to do. And, of course, she had to call at Portman Square to take her leave of Bruce and Phoebe and their family.

There was plenty to keep her busy, both mind and body. And she would not stay at home since she did not expect Piers to call yet knew that if she stayed, her eyes would be straying to the window and her ears listening for a knock on the door every minute—as they had done all through breakfast.

He would not come. Of course. He had other, more important matters to settle that morning. Besides, what was there to say? There was nothing at all.

She went shopping alone, and did not expect to see Piers anywhere on Oxford Street. Yet her stomach lurched every time she saw a tall, slim gentleman until she looked into his face and knew him to be a stranger.

It was a relief to arrive at Portman Square. Amanda was tearful at the thought of seeing her go, and even Mary hugged her and kissed her and told her that the two afternoons she had spent with Aunt Alice and Mr. Westhaven had been the most wonderful of her stay in London.

"Why does he call you Allie, Aunt Alice?" she asked.

"Because Uncle Web used to call me that," she said. "Have you forgotten?"

"I like it," the girl said. "May I call you Aunt Allie?"

And yet it was Piers who had first called her that, when she was fourteen and she had fallen in love with him with a girl's fierce passion.

"Allie of the braids," he had said outside church one Sunday, lightly tugging one of them. "Don't you ever sit on them by mistake?" And he had winked at her and moved on—to flirt with the eighteen-year-old Miss Roath, she could remember clearly. She had hated Miss Roath all that summer.

Even Richard and Jarvis seemed sorry to see her go. Bruce lamented the fact that she had not arrived sooner, when they had really needed her.

"I came as soon as I had your letter," she said. "And I think I was able to do something to cheer the children."

"It is a miracle they did not take a chill from being taken out so soon after their illness, though," Bruce said.

"They did not," Alice said briskly, "so you must not provoke yourself, Bruce."

"I do not know how I am to entertain Mary now that you are going, I am sure, Alice," Phoebe said.

"She has a nurse," Alice said. "And Jarvis is remarkably good-natured. I am sure he will agree to take her into the park occasionally or somewhere else amusing if you ask him, Phoebe."

"Well, I don't know, I am sure," her sister-in-law said. "What happened last night, Alice? Shocking goings-on, according to Amanda."

"The storm came on suddenly," Alice said. "Piers and Miss Borden were caught in the gardens and had to wait for it to pass before they could make a dash for the carriage."

"I daresay he had it all planned," Bruce said. "He never was quite respectable."

"I daresay he will be offering for her, then," Phoebe said. "Though I suppose he would have anyway. He has been paying her marked attention."

"Yes," Alice said.

"The girl's connection with trade is unfortunate," Phoebe said, "but of course her father was a baron. Mr. Westhaven might have done better for sure, but I suppose there will be a good dowry."

"I daresay you are right," Alice said.

"It is a pity in a way," Phoebe said. "I thought at one time that he fancied Amanda, but I daresay he thought her not good enough for him. He was always dreadfully high in the instep."

"I would not have given him Amanda anyway," Bruce said. "Ramshackle fellow. I never knew why Webster allowed him to be forever at Chandlos, Alice. Felt sorry for him, no doubt."

"Piers and Web were like brothers," Alice said quietly.

"Well, then," he said, "he might have had more respect for your good name, Alice, Papa having been who he was. I have not liked your association with him since you have been in town. It is a good thing you are returning to Bath, I believe."

"Yes," she said, rising from her chair, "I am looking forward to being at home again."

"Though what you find to do there I do not know," Bruce said. "And why pay to keep a house going for one person, Alice, when you could be with us and keeping yourself busy? Well, never let it be said that I did not offer you a brother's care."

"No," she said, crossing the room to him and kissing him on the cheek, "I will never let that be said, Bruce."

"You really ought not to be traveling with just a maid, Alice," Phoebe said. "What if you were attacked by highwaymen?"

"Then I suppose I would lose Web's diamonds and the coins in my purse," she said. "Don't worry about me, Phoebe. You have enough to worry about with Amanda's come-out."

"Yes," Phoebe said, turning her cheek for Alice's kiss, "you do not know what it is to be a mother, Alice. You have been very fortunate."

"Yes," Alice said, patting her sister-in-law's arm and turning to take her leave.

She could have been on her way to Bath a half hour or more before she was, she thought later, relaxing back in the seat of her carriage, a tearful Penelope at her side—there was a young groom in the house in London who would have to be found a position in Bath, Alice had begun to realize. She might have had at least a half hour longer of daylight for their travels that day. But she had sat longer than necessary over her luncheon, and then she had found it necessary to have her hair completely redone, though it was still tidy from the morning.

Well, she thought, closing her eyes, it was over now. There would be no more expecting him and not expecting him now. She would be able to gain control of herself and her life once more. She would be able to impose peace on herself again.

Except that there would never again be Piers or any hope that their friendship would bring them together again, even if only for brief days. For there was no more friendship and never would be again. She had had to make an instant decision when he had asked her if he might make love to her—not that he had put the request into words, of course. She had had to decide between one glorious night of love and a lifetime of friendship.

She had chosen the night of love.

And had been granted it. Oh, far more wonderfully than she had ever expected. She had never suspected— through nine years of a close and affectionate marriage she had never once suspected—that there could be such passion, such intense and shattering joy.

She had chosen her night of love and had lived through it. And now she must live through the rest of a lifetime without the friendship that had meant more to her than anything else in her life, though she had rarely seen him after Web's death.

Did she regret her decision? She had not yet given herself time to think fully, though she felt already a vast and frightening emptiness yawning ahead. Life was going to be dreadful indeed without Piers, especially after she had read the notice of his betrothal in the London papers. She would spend the rest of her life wondering about him, wondering if his marriage was bringing him any contentment, wondering if there were any children and how many and what genders.

She would wonder if he ever thought of her, ever blamed himself for coming to her for comfort and allowing her to give it. She would wonder if he ever suspected that it was her own need that had driven her to say yes to his question.

Oh, yes, she would regret her decision for a lifetime.

And yet for a lifetime she would have her night of love to remember. Piers kissing her as she had never been kissed, unclothing her in the candlelight, touching her with his mouth and his palms and his fingertips in places and in ways she had never been touched. Piers looking deeply into her eyes, unembarrassed by the intimacy they shared. Piers inside her, stroking her pain until it became an agony and then an ecstasy.

Piers holding her to him, rocking her against him, asking her to forgive him if she ever could.

Forgive him for giving her ecstasy?

She would never regret what had happened. She would never blame him. He had not come there to seduce her and had not done anything to her that was against her will. And she would never blame herself, either. She should do so, she knew. She had allowed a man into her house and into her bed the night before, and given him far more of herself than she had ever given her husband. What she had done would have been unthinkable to her just the day before. She should feel guilt and shame.

But she did not and she would not. She loved Piers, always had loved him and always would. He had needed her the night before—though doubtlessly today he felt both guilt and embarrassment—and she had given him all she had to give. She would not feel guilty for that.

Somehow she would live with the pain of the loss of his friendship. She had learned to live with losing Web, and in many ways that had been worse because he had been half of her daily life for nine years. She would learn to live with this loss, too. She could not say that she regretted having married Web just because the pain of his death was almost unbearable for a long time. In a similar way she would not say that she regretted sleeping with Piers just because there was pain to be dealt with again.

Life was worth the pain. The joys were worth the pain.

Two weeks later, Alice was wondering if such a feeling were not perhaps too unrealistic. It was hard to cope with pain, she was finding, by telling oneself that the joy preceding it had made it worthwhile.

Pain, simply stated, she was discovering anew, was painful.

At least she was happy that she had been able to get away from London. And happy that she had had a home in Bath to return to and a whole circle of friends glad to see her and eager to inquire after the health of her brother's family and to hear the news she brought from town.

She resumed her frequent visits to the Pump Room to talk with friends and to stroll indoors when the weather was bad. She visited the library and the shops on Milsom Street and the Abbey and the Upper Rooms and Sidney Park, usually with Andrea Potter, and entered once more into the lives of her friends, seeking to find forgetfulness of her own life.

Andrea teased her about Sir Clayton Lansing.

"He was like a fish lifted out of his tank once you had gone to London, Alice," she said. "It was most pitiful to behold, I do assure you. No one was surprised when he took himself off after you, claiming to be interested in the Season as a change from Bath for this spring. We were none of us deceived."

They both laughed.

"But did he make you an offer, Alice?" Andrea asked. "Do tell. All your friends have had a lively bet on it, I do assure you, though all of us wished to bet that he would. Did he?"

"Twice, I am afraid," Alice said. "Oh, Andrea, I do so hate to be disagreeable."

"It is my guess that you were not," Andrea said. "If you had been disagreeable the first time, he would not have asked the second, would he? You are just going to have to be a little more brutal, Alice, as I have told you before. A good kick in the shins ought to do it. The very idea that he is good enough for you!''

Alice laughed despite herself. "Perhaps I will not have to," she said. "He has not returned yet. Perhaps he has found someone in London who will receive his addresses more favorably."

"Oh. Who?" Andrea said scornfully.

Yes, it was good to be back, Alice decided. Good to have a home and friends, as she had not had when circumstances had forced her to leave Chandlos. She was well blessed.

Sometimes she almost had herself convinced. But if it had been true, perhaps her stomach would not have lurched quite so painfully when her housekeeper interrupted an afternoon visit that Andrea Potter was paying her with the announcement that a Mr. Piers Westhaven was waiting downstairs, asking if he could be admitted.

"Mr. Piers Westhaven?" Andrea said in some curiosity when the housekeeper had disappeared again to bring up the guest. "Alice, whoever have you been keeping secret from me, you wretch? You have turned as white as a ghost."

# 12

PIERS feared that he was losing his sense of humor. It was vastly diverting, he told himself numerous times during the two weeks following his betrothal, to watch the metamorphosis of a female from a young lady on the catch for a husband to a young lady successfully betrothed. Vastly diverting. Except that he could not force himself into feeling diverted, vastly or otherwise.

Cassandra—he had been given permission to call her that—was suddenly far too busy to grant him more than a very small portion of her time. Her days were given to endless shopping expeditions for her bride clothes and endless visiting with "friends," who had appeared largely nonexistent until the announcement of her engagement had appeared in the *Morning Post*.

When he was permitted to accompany her to some entertainment, she gave much of her attention to other admirers, the army of the disappointed. At a ball she could find a place for him on her dancing card only once each evening, and at the theater she could grant him only her divided attention during the performance; there were visitors to entertain in his box during the intervals. Other gentlemen, it seemed, were to be granted the exclusive right of driving her in the park during the fashionable hour of the afternoons.

"Mama has explained to me that it will not do to be seen to hang on your sleeve merely because you are my betrothed," she explained to him, all wide eyes, on one occasion. "It is not done."

Vastly amusing. Mr. Westhaven—his request to be

called by his given name had been ignored—could see that he was going to have to drag the girl, kicking and screaming and in chains, to Westhaven Park when the time came. All of which he would do—with the possible exception of the chains—he thought with unaccustomed grimness.

The marriage contract was not ready at the end of the one week. "We need to be doubly careful when there is a fortune at stake on each side, my dear sir, do we not?" Mr. Bosley had said by way of explanation. Not that Mr. Westhaven saw the necessity of a written contract anyway. He was obligated to marry the girl, his word had been given, and the announcement had been made. There was nothing more to be careful about as far as he was concerned.

Perhaps after all he might have been able to see the humor of the situation if circumstances had just been different. After all, there was no way on earth that he was going to allow a mere chit of a girl to tyrannize him once she was his wife. She would learn—and learn fast—that he would expect obedience once she had sworn to obey and that she must, for her own peace of mind, adjust herself to his way of life.

Perhaps he might have seen the humor. Perhaps not. Put that way, the vision of his future marriage made him look horribly the tyrant himself. Was that what he was going to do? Enforce obedience? Bend the girl to his will so that his own way of life would be undisturbed while her world would be turned upside down and inside out?

Devil take it, he was going to have to adjust to her, too, giving as much rein as he could allow while still remaining master of his own house.

She was not, after all, another Harriet. Harriet had catered to his selfishness. She had done all the bending, all the adjusting. And in return he had been fond of her. *Fond* of her! How magnanimous of him. How vastly generous. And he had gifted her with his child and killed her.

Damnation. There was no humor—none—in the situation. Or in life, either. It was all a vast joke that someone or something was playing on the human race. Except that it was not at all funny.

And there was that other thing, too—that thing that dominated his every waking moment and kept him from sleep at night and haunted his dreams when he did nod off.

There was Allie.

A grand, endless debate had been set up between two halves of his brain, and no inner judge had the sense to point out that the arguments had proceeded in circle upon circle upon endless circle and it was time to bring the debate to an end.

Given the great selfish sin he had committed against her, knowing that nothing could now recall that or put it right, had he done the right thing to let her go without a word or a letter? Was he right to leave it so, to disappear from her life? To leave her free to regain some peace of mind? Or did he owe it to her to see her, to make some explanation, some apology?

Was it selfishness only that made him want to see her one more time?

After two weeks the need had become an obsession. And finally he closed his mind to the half of his brain that told him seeing her was the worst thing he could do. He sent word to Russell Square that he must leave town for a few days, and took himself off to Bath and the York House hotel.

But suddenly, he discovered, the decision and the journey made, seeing her no longer seemed like a selfish obsession. Indeed, he would have given anything in the world, he thought as he got ready to call on her in Sidney Place—it had not been difficult to discover where she lived—to call out his carriage again and make for the London road.

How would he face her? How would he look her in the eye? How would he greet her? What would he say?

But having come this far, he must call on her. Perhaps it was the wrong thing to do, but he must do it now or live in torment for the rest of his life. Perhaps he could put it all behind him once he had spoken to her and made some sort of atonement.

And perhaps the moon would fall from the sky, too.

There was no time to prepare herself, no time to answer Andrea's question. He was striding through the doorway almost as soon as her housekeeper had gone out through it. He was coming across the room to her, both hands outstretched, looking so very familiar, so very much Piers—had she expected him to have changed in two weeks? Her own hands, she was surprised to see, were stretched out, too.

"Allie," he said, and took her hands in a strong, almost bruising clasp.

"Piers." She returned pressure for pressure.

She thought he was going to come all the way to her and kiss her, but he checked himself, glanced at Andrea, and smiled—Piers in every way.

"Andrea," she said, "may I present Mr. Piers Westhaven, my husband's dearest friend? Mrs. Andrea Potter, Piers."

He bowed, she inclined her head. Both looked amused for some reason.

"You were Mr. Penhallow's friend?" Andrea said. "You have not seen Alice, then, since his passing? She is doing very well, is she not, and is quite indispensable to us here in Bath, sir."

"We met in London recently," he said, "and played uncle and aunt to Allie's younger niece on a few occasions. I happen to be in Bath for a few days, Allie, and decided that I must call on you."

"Splendid!" Andrea said. Her expression was still one of amusement, Alice saw. "My husband and I are entertaining a few friends this evening for cards and conversation and supper. You must accompany Alice, if you will, sir."

He bowed. "Thank you, ma'am," he said. "But I am not certain of my plans, or of Allie's."

"I read the announcement of your betrothal in the

*Post,* Piers,'' Alice said. "Please accept my congratulations.''

"Yes,'' he said. "Thank you.''

Andrea's look of disappointment was almost comical, Alice thought.

Andrea got to her feet decisively. "Well,'' she said, "I must proceed on my way to the library, Alice. I am pleased to have made your acquaintance, Mr. Westhaven. I shall see both of you tonight?''

"Thank you, ma'am,'' Mr. Westhaven said.

"Yes,'' Alice said at the same moment.

And suddenly they were stranded in the room together, she turned toward the door, having watched her friend on her way, he somewhere behind her. She composed her face, clasped her hands loosely in front of her, and turned.

"Piers—'' she said.

"Allie—''

They had spoken simultaneously.

"Sit down,'' she said, indicating a chair and taking one across from it, "and tell me what you are doing here just two weeks after your betrothal.''

He sat down. "I came to see what is so wonderful about Bath that you would wish to make it your permanent home,'' he said. "I have not been here for years. It is quite splendid in the sunshine, is it not? I thought I might take the waters for a few days to see if they will improve my good sense. Do they do that, Allie, or do they work only on physical ailments?''

"I think they are all a big hoax,'' she said.

"Oh, don't say that above a whisper,'' he said. "You might drive all the visitors away, Allie, and be doomed to spend the rest of your life in company with the remaining five inhabitants.''

"Why did you come?'' she asked.

He grinned. "It is obviously a long time since you prepared for your own wedding, Allie,'' he said. "You must have forgotten just how many hours and days you had to spend in conference with your dressmaker and milliner and fan maker and everyone else. And how much time you must spend with your disappointed suitors. As the mere husband-to-be, my presence in London at the moment is supremely redundant. I will not be needed again until the wedding day.''

"Will it be soon?" she asked.

"The date has not been set," he said. "It is a very ticklish matter, as I am sure you will appreciate. A fine balance has to be struck between not holding it too soon and thus wasting a few moments of the Season and not holding it too late and finding that the crème de la crème has withdrawn already and will not return for the celebrations. It would be a great shame to waste a grand wedding on only half the *ton*, now, would it not?"

"Piers," she said.

"I am to be congratulated, you know, Allie," he said. "It turns out that I am not marrying a mindless little bundle of sweet innocence after all, but a young lady with very much a mind of her own. Did you suspect it? It should be an interesting marriage, should it not?"

"Piers," she said. "Don't."

"One great injustice has been done me, though," he said. "My mother disapproves. Can you imagine, Allie? I agreed to take on a leg-shackle and fill the nursery at Westhaven all so that she might become a doting grandmama, and she disapproves."

"Has she said so?" Alice asked.

"Oh, she doesn't need to." He drummed his fingers on the arm of his chair. "I took her to tea at Russell Square, and she addressed one remark to Cassandra. She conversed for the rest of the time with Bosley and Lady Margam. I believe Cassandra has made up her mind that Mama will not set foot over the threshold of Westhaven once we are married. She did not say so in quite those words, but I foresee an interesting conflict developing in the future. Can you see my mother being kept from her grandchildren?"

"Piers," she said.

"If there *are* grandchildren," he said. "I daresay

Cassandra is made of far sterner stuff than Harriet was, but I might succeed in killing her just the same, don't you think, Allie?''

"Piers!" She was on her feet and crossing the room to the window. "Don't!"

"But it is all vastly diverting, don't you see?" He was on his feet, too, some distance behind her. "And very much my just deserts, Allie. I set myself to choosing a bride much as I did the first time, with very little thought to the young lady concerned and her wishes. I mean, what young girl in her right mind would wish to ally herself freely to a man of six-and-thirty? I was the only one who mattered. I would choose someone who would interfere with my life in almost no way. Some little mouse like Harriet. Someone whose sole function would be to breed my heirs and live through the experience. I have been justly served. I deserve Cassandra. And perhaps she deserves me, too.''

Alice rested her forehead against the glass of the window. "I care about you, Piers," she said. "I care about your happiness.''

There was a short silence. Then he laughed. "You care about me?" he said. "After what I did to you, Allie? You don't wish me in the hottest flame of hell?''

"You did not do anything to me," she said. "What we did, we did together. We needed each other. You needed comfort for the unexpected disaster of the evening. I needed comfort for—well, for a two-year loneliness. We chose to comfort each other in the wrong way, but we chose it together, Piers. You do not need to take the burden of guilt all on yourself.''

"You are Web's wife," he said quietly.

"No." She raised one hand to draw invisible patterns on the glass. "I am Web's widow, Piers.''

"God," he said from behind her. "God, Allie, what did I do? You have always been on a pedestal for me. I have always marveled that you would condescend to accept my friendship. I always wondered at the perfection of the love you and Web shared. Oh, God. And I defiled you.''

She imposed calmness on herself with one deeply indrawn breath and turned to face him.

''Then you have discovered after all,'' she said, ''that I am human, that I am a woman with needs. You satisfied one of those needs for me on that one night, Piers. That is all. It was nothing more significant or more dreadful than that. I was a widow of two years. I needed physical love. You gave it to me.''

She kept her clasped hands still and relaxed. She kept her eyes steadily on his. His own closed briefly.

''I did not ravish you?'' he said.

''Piers,'' she said. ''You know you did not.''

''I have not destroyed you?'' he said. ''I pictured you living in a torment of guilt and remorse, Allie. And hatred of me. I thought I had destroyed you.''

Somehow her facial muscles obeyed her will and she smiled. ''Well,'' she said, ''it is a good thing you came, then. You can see that it is not so. Is that what you have been doing to yourself, poor Piers? Have you been torturing your conscience?''

''Yes,'' he said. ''I did not know if I should stay out of your life permanently or if I should come to try to make some sort of peace with you. Allie, forgive me. Whatever you say, it was my fault. I had no business calling on you at that hour. Say you forgive me.''

''If it will make you feel better and stop you from tormenting yourself, then yes,'' she said, forcing herself forward one step, willing her hands to steadiness as she stretched them out to him. ''You are forgiven, Piers.''

He took her hands and bowed his head over them. He began to raise one of them to his lips, but he lowered it again. He released her hands after squeezing them tightly.

''And how do I ask forgiveness of Web?'' His smile was a little twisted.

''You don't,'' she said. ''I was never, ever unfaithful to Web, and would not have been if we had both lived to a great old age. And you never dishonored him and would not have done were he still living, even if you and I had been alone under very tempting circumstances, as we were two weeks ago. We both know that, Piers. Neither of us has wronged Web in any way at all.''

''Do you miss him dreadfully?'' he asked.

''Sometimes,'' she said. ''Come and sit down again, Piers, and tell me about your betrothal. Is it quite impossible?''

''Perhaps not impossible,''he said. ''Improbable, though. I am going to have to work like the devil at my marriage, Allie, so that we do not come to hate each other.''

''One always does,'' she said. ''Have to work at a marriage, that is.''

''Did you and Web?'' he asked. ''You seemed always to be the perfect couple.''

''I resented his worshipful attitude,'' she said. ''He resented the fact that I would not allow him to do everything for me, even breathe. He would not even allow me another child after Nicholas died. We both had to learn to give a little and to laugh at ourselves.''

''Perhaps Cassandra will be good for me,'' he said. ''She certainly will not allow me to have my own way all the time, as Harriet did. I will have to learn a little bit of selflessness. Do you think it possible, Allie? Am I quite beyond redemption, do you think?''

''But will it be one-sided?'' she asked. ''Will she be willing to give in to you sometimes, Piers?''

''She is very young,'' he said. ''Little more than a child, Allie. The very young are entitled to be more selfish than men in their dotage, like me. I think perhaps I am going to have to devote myself to making her happy. That will be a new venture for me. Something to brighten up life.'' He grinned.

''Oh,'' she said with a sigh, ''it does not sound promising. And how very rag-mannered of me to say that aloud. But I do so want you to be happy, Piers. Web used to say that you had a great capacity for happiness and contentment and love if you could just find what you were searching for.''

"Yes, well," he said with a flashing smile, "I might have had a large brood to romp with at Westhaven now, Allie, if Harriet had only had the good sense to remain alive. Poor Harriet. I wish I could go back and relive that marriage. I would make an effort to bring some happiness into her life before forcing her into doing her duty, as the bearing of heirs seems to be viewed. Perhaps she would have liked to travel.''

"Harriet was very happy just to be married to you and living at Westhaven Park," she said. "And she was quite ecstatic to find herself increasing after or a few months. She was shy with me. The only time . can remember her being eloquent was on the subject of her pregnancy and her excitement at being able to bear you a child. She was happy, Piers. Don't start to doubt that fact again. I thought Web had set you straight on that long ago.''

He shrugged and smiled. "She was a sweet girl, wasn't she?" he said. "Far better than I deserved. Have you heard about your niece? No, probably not. It seems that she is now sighing over a Mr. Latham, who does not know she exists. Mr. King made the lamentable mistake of showing interest in her as soon as she showed it in him. Gossip has it that he committed the incredible faux pas of offering for her last week. Her interest in him died an instant death, of course.''

"Well," Alice said, "she is very young still, Piers, and rather giddy. I am sure it will be best if she does not fix her choice for another year or two yet, when perhaps she will have grown up a little.''

"I imagine the estimable Bruce will have a thing or two to say if he has to take her back to the country for the summer unattached," he said. "Think of all the waste of a fortune, Allie.''

"Phoebe will take it as a personal failure," she said.

There was a sudden lull in the conversation, and they smiled rather uncertainly at each other.

"Are we still friends?" he asked. "Or are you wishing me to the devil, Allie?"

"I don't think two people can decide not to be friends when they have been friends forever," she said. "I would miss you, Piers. There would be too much of a void in my life."

"And in mine," he said. "It has been almost unbearable in the past two weeks. You would have come home to Bath anyway, and I would have been missing you and knowing that perhaps I would not see you again for a long time. But there is a difference between thinking of an absent friend and thinking of someone who used to be a friend and never will be again. Imagine the embarrassment of meeting by accident some years down the road."

"I'm glad you came," she said and smiled.

"I could return to London today," he said. "Or I could stay for a few days. If I leave immediately, we may find ourselves just as embarrassed when we meet next. If I stay, we can spend some time together and reestablish our friendship as it has always been. Of course, my staying may be distressing or offensive to you. Tell me what to do, Allie."

She looked into his half-smiling face. If he left, she could keep working on building her life of dull contentment, as she had for the past year, but with the added happiness of knowing that he had come to make his peace with her. If he left, she could readjust herself more quickly. If he stayed, there would be all the more pain when he left again, all the greater difficulty in adjusting to life in a place where he had been with her.

But once he left, whether now or in a few days' time, she would not see him again before his marriage to Cassandra Borden. And she would not wish to see him after that. She would always consider herself his friend, but she would not want to see him again.

The next few days were all she could ever have of him. And temptation, as she had found on one previous occasion, is the most difficult of all temptations to resist.

"Stay," she said. "Andrea will be disappointed if you fail to appear in her drawing room this evening. There are not many new visitors at this time of year, you know."

He rose to his feet. "I shall dress in all my London finery then," he said, "and dazzle the ladies, shall I, Allie? May I take you up in my carriage?"

"Yes," she said. "And I shall dress in my London finery, too, Piers, so that you will not outdazzle me."

He grinned. "I could not do that even if you dressed in rags, Allie," he said. "Until this evening, then."

He bowed to her, spoiled the effect by winking, and left the room.


During the same afternoon at the Russell Square house in London, Mr. Bosley was talking with his niece while Lady Margam was otherwise engaged.

"Well, Cass," he said heartily, rubbing his hands together. "We will have the marriage contract all drawn up for Mr. Westhaven's signature when he returns from the country. Though, of course, the word of a gentleman is to be trusted anyway. Gentlemen are not like cutthroat businessmen." He laughed merrily. "And are you happy, girl?"

"Yes, Uncle," she said.

"It is strange how gentlemen think to pull the wool over everyone's eyes," he said. "A little investigation can uncover some strange things, Cass."

She looked inquiringly at him.

"Sir Clayton Lansing," he said, "who has been somewhat attentive, Cassie. Do you like him, eh?"

"I am betrothed to Mr. Westhaven, Uncle," she said demurely.

He laughed heartily. "And that means you cannot like any other gentleman, of course," he said. "Sir Clayton is not as wealthy as he has made out. You have had a fortunate escape, wouldn't you say, Cass?"

"If you say so, Uncle," she said, uncertain of his tone.

"Of course," he said, "there is a quite extensive estate. Very rundown, so I have heard, and heavily mortgaged. Gentlemen are strange creatures. They think such a fact something to hide. They don't know where their assets lie. Would you like your uncle to purchase the mortgage, Cass?"

Cassandra did not know the correct answer and wisely kept her mouth shut.

"It is done already," he said. "His grandfather is a viscount, Cassie. Did you know that?"

"I believe he mentioned it once, Uncle," she said. "But Sir Clayton's father was a younger son."

"There were three sons," Mr. Bosley said, "and two grandsons. Hordes of granddaughters, but they don't count for anything. Two grandsons, Cass, and one of them dying of consumption. Not Lansing. All three sons are dead, by the way, and the grandfather doddering on the edge of the grave." He chuckled.

"Poor gentleman," Cassandra said.

Mr. Bosley chuckled again. "The soft hearts of females!" he said. "Lansing probably don't even know about the sad state of health of his cousin. The family had a falling-out years ago. Maybe you rushed into your betrothal, Cassie."

"Yes, Uncle," she said.

"Ah, well," he said heartily, "it is too late now, Cass. We cannot let the gentleman down now that the announcements have been made, can we? Your mother would not consider it at all the thing."

"No, Uncle," she said.

"You must forget what I have told you, then," he said with a sigh. "You must certainly do nothing to fix the man's interest now, Cassie. You must be a good girl."

"Yes, Uncle," she said.

"A pity, though,' he said. "His assets and mine

combined, Cass. Ah, well, Mr. Westhaven will be a baron one day, though the present baron is said to be in excellent health and is a relatively young man. He could live another twenty years.''

# 13

MR. WESTHAVEN did not after all wear his best London finery that evening. His shirt did not have quite the quantity of lace at the wrists that he would wear to a London ball, and he instructed his disappointed valet that a simple knotting of his neckcloth would be more appropriate than any of the more artistic creations the man had been perfecting over the past few months. And he chose a coat more to be comfortable in than to give the impression that it had been painted on him.

He combed his hair and wished he had not given in to the whim to be fashionable. A Brutus style could not be disguised as anything more casual. The only thing it did show off was the fact that he had not lost any of his hair, even at the temples. A fine vanity, to want to display that phenomenon.

He had become quite the town dandy, he thought in disapproval. He wanted to be himself again. Except that there was no being himself ever again. There was Cassandra to marry and the rest of his life to devote to her happiness. If it could be done. If he could change himself that much. And there was his love for Allie to be hidden from everyone and everything but his own heart. Not that there was anything particularly new about that. He had done it for years and had had such great success that eventually he had been able to hide the truth even from himself.

Maybe he would be as fortunate again, he thought, as he rode in his carriage to Sidney Place.

He was, of course, going about the thing in a mar-

velously illogical manner. He had accomplished what
he had hoped to do that afternoon—and far more than
he had expected. At best he had expected to win her
forgiveness and set her mind at rest about the extent
of her own guilt. He had not dared to hope that their
friendship could somehow emerge battered but unbro-
ken from the stress they—he—had put upon it.

So he had accomplished his aim and more. He
should be on his way back to London now, on his way
back to his future. He should be accepting reality, the
knowledge that though he and Allie still professed to
be friends, in fact they would not meet again except
by accidental circumstance. Instead he had suggested
that he stay for a few days—in order that their friendship be set on a firmer footing again. From what airy
castle had he drawn that strange excuse for staying?

What could be accomplished by his remaining in
Bath? Pain, that was what. He must enjoy inflicting
pain on himself. For he would see her for a few days,
meet her friends, talk with her, laugh with her, perhaps delude himself into feeling that those days would
last forever and fall more deeply in love with her.

If that were possible. He did not think anyone was
capable of loving more than he loved Allie. Despite
all his terrible embarrassment when he called on her
that afternoon, one look at her had brought on that
familiar sensation of homecoming. She had looked so
very much herself—had he expected her to be different
after two weeks?—slim, graceful, elegant, beautiful,
and self-possessed. She had been a little pale maybe,
but she had smiled and reached out her hands for his—
had he held his out first? He could not remember.

All the world had been reaching out to him, and he
had taken her hands in his and known he was at home
again. He would have taken her right into his arms and
folded her to himself if he had not become suddenly
aware that there was someone else in the room. Thank
heaven for Mrs. Andrea Potter at that moment!

It had been as he thought, then, as he had discovered after Mrs. Potter had taken her leave. Allie in her

usual calm and sensible manner had been quite open
and forthright about it. He had come to her late at
night in her own apartments, when she was already in
her nightclothes. His male presence had awoken a
hunger in her that had not been satisfied since Web
died—women were unfortunate not to be able to satisfy their hungers as easily as men could. He had been
there, and she had given in to a momentary weakness
and taken him into her bed.

There was nothing to blame in that. He would not
begin to blame her. Indeed, he felt an ache of sympathy for the emptiness of her life as a widow. There
was no blame in what she had done. But there was no
love, either.

He laughed softly to himself as the carriage came to
a stop outside the house on Sidney Place. Had he
hoped, against all logic and sense, to find her broken
and distraught with love for him? It was extremely
fortunate for both of them that she was not.

"Allie," he said a few minutes later, "you simply
must let me return to York House to change. No one
will even notice me once they have glanced at you."

She laughed. "Absurd!" she said. "Bath will gob-
ble you up, Piers—a gentleman below the age of fifty
and handsome into the bargain. And it is not even the
Bath Season."

"Well," he said, "I was very successful in drawing
that compliment from you, was I not? Thank you,
ma'am. And who was sensible enough to tell you that
you look superb in that shade of dark green, Allie?
You wore it in London a few times, though I have
never seen that particular gown before."

"My eyes told me," she said. "I like the color."

"Very sensible eyes," he said, ushering her out onto
the street with a hand at the small of her back, and
handing her into his carriage. "There are to be cards
this evening? Will there be any dowager duchesses to
separate from their fortunes?"

"There seems to be rather a dearth of dowager

duchesses in Bath these days,'' she said. ''A lamentable fact. The city is not what it used to be, alas.''

''Hm,'' he said. ''Some dowager marchionesses, then?''

She shook her head.

''Countesses? Viscountesses? Baronesses? Good Lord, Allie, this is not to be a dull, respectable party, is it?''

''I am afraid so,'' she said. ''This is Bath, Piers, where the rules do not permit one to play deep even if there are fortunes to be won and lost.''

''And what do you people do for enjoyment?'' he said. ''Converse? Dance? Walk? Ride? Drink tea?''

''And gossip and drink the waters,'' she said. ''The really brave even bathe in them.''

''And no gambling,'' he said.

''And no gambling.''

''Well,'' he said, ''I call this a very poor-spirited place, Allie, if a man cannot experience the excitement of not knowing when he recovers from his hangover in the morning whether he is still in possession of his fortune and estate or not. Where is the challenge in living?''

''Shocking, is it not?'' she said.

They were both chuckling then, and he reached for her hand and took it in a warm clasp. Until he realized what he had done and released it again. He turned hastily to the window and leaned forward.

''I must say,'' he said, ''I am thankful not to be a horse in Bath. For that matter, I suppose I am thankful not to be a horse anywhere. But I really would not fancy hauling carriages up these hills, would you, Allie?''

''I suppose this particular team is fortunate that we do not weigh two tons apiece,'' she said.

''Good Lord!'' he said. ''Have you been eating any creamy pastries lately, Allie?''

''No,'' she said. ''I have found them almost easy to resist without an impudent gentleman to place them right on my plate.''

"Well," he said. "That situation can be rectified over the next few days. If all you need is a little temptation, then I am here at your service to provide it, ma'am."

The next moment he was leaning forward again and asking if they were almost at Brock Street, though he knew exactly where Brock Street was and how far away from it they were. Devil take it, had he really spoken that last sentence out loud? He must have because Allie behind him was busily drawing a word map of the upper portion of Bath as if it were of the utmost importance to both of them.

It was very much the usual sort of evening in Bath. Alice had experienced dozens just like it during the year she had lived there. Andrea was her usual talkative self. Mr. Potter, as usual, said scarcely a word and yet was a comfortable, smiling gentleman to whom people liked to talk. Colonel and Mrs. Smithers were there, always very much together. Miss Lavinia Horvath had come with her brother, even though she had just returned from a visit to their sister, who had recently given birth to her fifth child. Miss Dean had brought Sir Harold, her father, though he rarely went out these days unless the distance was very short and the weather mild. Mr. and Mrs. Wainwright had come though it was their twenty-fourth wedding anniversary and they had considered giving their own party.

"But who would have come," Mr. Wainwright said, "when all our friends are here? Twenty-four years ago we might have welcomed the prospect of a party for two, but this year my wife welcomes the company, I would wager."

Mrs. Wainwright flushed and looked reproachfully at him.

It was all very much the same as usual. The Smithers, Sir Harold, and Miss Horvath settled to a quiet game of cards while the rest of them conversed. And during tea Miss Dean played to them on the spinet and even sang a couple of songs.

Except that it was not at all a usual evening. And not at all the same as any of those dozens of similar evenings that had gone before. For Piers was there, too, and his presence made a whole universe of difference.

And it was not just to her. The whole company seemed cheered by the introduction of a visitor. And Piers, smiling, handsome, and charming, became an instant favorite with every conversational group. He even turned the pages of music for Miss Dean, who usually did the job for herself.

He did not stay at her side, Alice was both relieved and disappointed to find. She was mainly relieved. The carriage ride had been something of a strain. They had succeeded very well in keeping their conversation light and bantering, but there had been those awkward moments. It would be better by far not to risk any more of those under the scrutiny of so many eyes.

Andrea sat beside her when everyone else was otherwise engaged.

"I was afraid Mr. Westhaven would not come," she said. "It would have been a waste, would it not, Alice, for such a gorgeous gentleman to spend the evening alone at York House?"

Alice smiled. "Piers enjoys company," she said.

"Alice." Andrea reached out and patted her hand briefly. "Never let it be said I am the inquisitive sort, my dear, but I am positively dying of curiosity. Who in the world is he? And don't tell me he was your late husband's dearest friend. Perhaps he was, but I am talking in the present tense. Who is he?"

"He was our neighbor," Alice said calmly. "From Westhaven Park. He was our friend. And he is my friend."

"Piers," Andrea said, "and Allie. Just friends, Alice? For a moment this afternoon I thought you were about to fly into each other's arms. I wished I could have melted into the furniture so that you would forget all about my presence. Alas, your Mr. Westhaven noticed me. And smiled. He has one of those smiles that have the strange effect of turning the beholder's knees weak. What is going on, Alice?''

''Nothing is going on,'' Alice said. ''Piers and Web were always like brothers, even from childhood. Piers and I are like brother and sister. That is all, Andrea. You must not look for a grand romance, you know, however much you always enjoy it between the pages of a book. Did you not hear me congratulate him on his betrothal?''

Andrea pulled a face. ''I suppose she is a sweet young thing half his age,'' she said. ''What a shame to waste all that gorgeous masculinity on a green girl. I am making you blush, Alice. And I am being quite ill-mannered, pressing you when you clearly have decided to tell me nothing of any significance. Alas for good manners. I would like to shake more information from you. Have you seen the new bonnets at Darnell's? Very tempting confections. You must come with me to see them tomorrow.''

''Yes,'' Alice said, greeting this new topic of conversation eagerly. ''I need some new kid gloves, too.''

She talked all evening and to most of the guests in turn. They were all her acquaintances and friends. Sir Harold asked her with a wink, just before having to pause for a lengthy coughing spell, when that rogue Lansing would be back to cut him out from her affections again. Mrs. Smithers asked her how ladies were wearing their hair in London this spring. Mr. Potter listened to her description of the galleries she had seen in town. Miss Horvath compared notes with her on the joys and trials of looking after a relative's young children.

And every moment there was the sameness and the difference, the dull comfort of the usual routine and the exciting difference of the one detail.

For Piers was there, and try as she would to relax into the security of home and friends, she was aware of him every moment. And occasionally she caught his eye and they would both smile. A couple of times he winked at her, when he thought and she hoped that no one was observing them.

After the first hour she gave up the attempt to ignore his presence or to pretend to herself that nothing was really different at all. She would not ignore him or the effect he was having on her evening. Indeed, she would deliberately do the opposite, she decided before the evening was out, both on that occasion and during the few days to come before he returned to London.

This was all she would ever have of him, and she was going to enjoy these few days for all they were worth. She would enjoy them in the strict privacy of her heart, without either Piers or anyone else being at all aware of her reason for doing so.

He was a friend, a dear friend, spending a few days in Bath and some time with her. There was nothing indecorous about that, even if he was a newly betrothed man. There would be nothing indecorous. Just two friends enjoying each other's company for perhaps a few hours of each day. Only she would know that she was grasping at a little more time, just a few more days of time, with her lover.

For she loved him as she always had. That had not changed, of course, and never would. But there was more than that now, as she had discovered that afternoon as soon as he had walked through the door into her drawing room. He had been her lover for one brief night, and now she was aware of him in a far more physical sense than she ever had been before.

She knew him now. The biblical word was very apt. She had known him before, had felt very close to him, had felt that she understood him better than he understood himself. And she had loved him before, ached for him, wanted his happiness. But she knew him fully now. Oh, there were still mysteries. One could never know every shadowed corner of another person. Even she and Web, close as they had been, had not known each other completely. He had never known how much of her heart belonged to his friend. And if he had not known that about her, what had she not known about him?

And the same was true of Piers. They lived quite separate lives. They had been intimate on only that one occasion. But she knew him, nevertheless. She knew him with her body to the deepest core of her femininity. And she knew him with her love and with her friendship.

Soon she would know him only in memory. Soon she would lose him. But now, for a few days, she would be able to see him, talk with him, laugh with him. She would not be able to touch him or look at him as she wished or say any of the things she wished. But that did not matter. Piers had only ever been for her remotest dreams, anyway. In the event, she had had far more of him than she had ever hoped for.

She would make it enough, these few days. She would take him to all the places she loved best. And for the rest of her life there would be memories of him there, in the place where she lived. The pain would dull eventually. It always did. The pain of losing Web had dulled and left pleasant memories behind. The same would happen with Piers. For weeks, perhaps months, she would wish he had never come. But after that—she must impose patience on her aching heart— there would be pleasure in memories.

She would live for that time—once he had gone. But he had not gone yet. And perhaps he would stay for three or four days. Perhaps even for a week. She would not think of it. She would live and enjoy one day at a time.

"I suppose you put in an appearance at the Pump Room at seven o'clock each morning, Allie?" Piers said when his carriage was taking them home later. "You don't sit in the waters up to your neck, by any chance, do you?"

"Gracious, no!" she said.

"Glad I am to hear it," he said. "I should have felt obliged to do likewise. And I think I would feel remarkably silly holding a conversation with you with only our heads showing above water, Allie.''

She laughed. ''I usually arrive at eight o'clock rather than seven,'' she said.

''Glad I am to hear that, too,'' he said. ''Though even the thought of being out of my bed by eight gives me the shudders.''

''Then you must have changed,'' she said. ''I can recall numerous occasions when you dragged Web off shooting even before the crack of dawn.''

''Ah,'' he said. ''My salad days. I like your friends, by the way, Allie. Solid citizens, all.''

''Do I detect a tone of sarcasm?'' she asked. ''There is nothing wrong with being a solid citizen, Piers.''

''Maligned again,'' he said, taking her hand in his. ''No, I was not being sarcastic, my suspicious friend. Sometimes I can be serious, you know. I like them. Mrs. Potter is your particular friend? I am glad. She has a gleam of mischief in her eyes. The octogenarian fancies you. Did you know that?''

''Sir Harold?'' she said. ''He is a dear. He enjoys flirting with me and any other unattached lady he sets eyes on. He does not set eyes on many, as he rarely goes out these days. I call on him and Miss Dean at least once a week. She leads a rather lonely life.''

His hand removed itself unobtrusively from hers. They rode the rest of the way to Sidney Place in silence.

''I will see you in the morning, Allie?'' he asked as he helped her down from the carriage. ''You do not mind? You would not prefer that I take myself off back to London?''

''No,'' she said. ''If you wish to stay, Piers, then I am quite happy. Good night.''

She squeezed his hand, which she had taken when descending the steps of his carriage, released it, and turned to the door of her house, which her housekeeper was holding open for her.

''Good night, Allie,'' he said.

\* \* \*

Piers had slept well. Despite the fact that he was up and walking briskly about the streets of Bath by seven o'clock, he had slept well. More deeply and dreamlessly than he had slept since the night he had stayed with Alice.

He had been careful the evening before to reestablish their friendship. He had kept conversation between them light; he had stayed away from her at the Potters' house, busying himself with making himself agreeable to her friends. On the whole, he had done rather well, he thought, despite the few slips.

The thing was that they really were friends, that he really was comfortable with her once he started to talk to her. And it always seemed the most comfortable thing in the world to take her hand in his when he was beside her. He had done it often in London, he could recall. He would have to be careful of that. It must not happen again.

But on the whole he was pleased. He did not think either she or anyone else would have realized how everything that was himself had been focused on her last evening, aware of her, wanting her, loving her. And feeling the irrepressible guilt at his own selfishness.

But he had put that guilt finally to rest last night before he lay down to sleep. She had been cheerful and contented all evening. The only time she had shown discomfort was when he had made that ghastly teasing statement about being her tempter. She had been happy with her friends, happy to have him there. But not especially happy to be with him. She would have been as content without him, among her other friends.

He was nothing to her beyond a friend. He *was* that. There was no doubt about the fact that she was dearly fond of him. But nothing more than that. Despite what had happened between them, his presence did not distress her. He would not be harming her by staying for a few days. If he had had any doubt, her tone of quiet assurance as she had said good night to him the evening before had finally convinced him.

He would be harming no one by staying. Not her and not Cassandra. He was not having any sort of affair with Allie. Once he was married to Cassandra, he would probably never see Allie again. And even if he did, there would be no question of his being unfaithful. If there was one value he believed in more than any other, it was fidelity in marriage. Even his love for Allie would be ruthlessly suppressed once he had vowed to love and cherish Cassandra.

There were just these few days when he would content himself with being a friend. He would feel no guilt. Indeed, doubtless he would be doing Allie good by staying. She would remember him as a friend. The memory of what they had become for one brief night would be displaced by what they had always been to each other.

He was the only one who would suffer. And even that was questionable. How could he suffer from spending a last few days with the woman he loved more dearly than life itself?

And so he allowed himself the great selfishness, and made it greater by not forcing himself to stay away from her the next day. After talking with her and her friends for a few minutes in the Pump Room, he drew her away to stroll about the room with him.

"After all, Allie," he said, "this is what is done, is it not? One cannot come to Bath and not promenade in the Pump Room. When in Bath, do as the Bathians do, I say. Or is it Bathans? Or Bathonians?"

"I always say the people of Bath," she said.

"The voice of common sense," he said. "Do look at that lady's face, Allie. Do you suppose she is enjoying the water?"

"Absolutely," she said. "The more horrid it tastes, you know, and the more it makes the drinker contort his face, the more good it is doing."

"Ah," he said. "You should have been a man, Allie. You might have been a physician."

"Perhaps one day," she said, "there will be women physicians. Now, there is a thought for you."

"I would be ailing for the rest of my days," he said. "If she turned out to be as pretty as you, of course."

"Perhaps we have an interesting theory here," she said, "for the fact that women tend to suffer poor health far more than men."

"Ah," he said. "Philosophy at eight in the morning, Allie? Too heavy, my dear. Now, what do you think of the yellow waistcoat on the rotund gentleman by the window? Rather loud, would you say?"

"Deafening," she agreed.

# 14

PIERS stayed in Bath for three more days, days during which neither he nor Alice thought about their coming separation, days during which they thought of nothing else. They grasped at the moment with a desperate sort of determination, each outwardly calm and cheerful, each content that the other would not suffer at all at the end.

On that first morning when they came out of the Pump Room, each with the intention of returning home for breakfast, Alice invited him into the Abbey, which was right beside the old Roman baths and the Pump Room. It was her favorite place in Bath, and she wanted to have future associations of him with the church.

"My stomach may make noisy objections and get itself evicted by morning worshipers," he said, "but the spirit is very willing, Allie. It is so many years since I have been inside that I cannot even remember what it looks like."

It was a splendid stone structure, massive, high and cool, its large stained glass windows saving it gloriously from gloom. It was one of those churches in which one felt instantly the presence of God and in which one instinctively lowered one's voice to a whisper even when there was no service in progress.

"Ah, yes," he said, pausing at the end of the nave and gazing down toward the altar, "I remember now. All the power and majesty of God, and man's insignificance."

They walked about the Abbey in near silence and

sat down finally on two chairs close to the front. Alice remained sitting even when her companion knelt on the kneeler, his arms resting loosely over the back of the chair before him.

She watched him and wondered how many people in his life had thought they knew him, and had taken the wit, the humor, the apparently casual attitude to life as the whole man. How many people thought Piers was a man of surface charm and little depth of character?

She loved the witty, lighthearted Piers. He was a joy to be with. But she was not sure she would have loved him as she did if that had been the whole of him. But there was this side to his character, too, which few people knew. She had seen it for as long as she had known him. Most recently she had seen it in London at the galleries they had visited together. And now here.

It was lovely to talk to Piers, to be entertained by him, to match wits with him. It was just as lovely to be silent with him, when that silence could be a mutually felt and a peaceful thing. She would never have brought him to this particular place if she had for one moment feared that he would joke about it or even talk endlessly about it.

She could happily sit there in silence all morning, all day, she thought. But he sat up beside her again after a while and turned to smile at her. His shoulder touched hers briefly, and his right hand moved across, rested awkwardly for a few moments against the outside of his leg, and then returned to twine fingers with the other hand in his lap. His shoulder moved away from hers.

Ah, he had grown self-conscious, she thought sadly. He had held her hand several times in London and twice the evening before, always as a spontaneous and casual gesture of affection. But he had become aware that any physical touch might be misconstrued and could be potentially dangerous. He would not touch her again.

It was something she regretted. She would have liked to rest her shoulder against his, to have her hand in his warm clasp. Not for any sensual reason. It was neither the time nor the place for that sort of craving. But merely because they were sharing the wonder and the majesty of the Abbey, and it would have felt lovely to have done so with more than just their minds. She kept her own hands clasped loosely in her lap and closed her eyes.

And Piers beside her ached for the same closeness and turned his head to smile at her again. But she was in her own world, her chin lifted, her eyes closed. Beautiful, serene, unattainable Allie.

He looked upward to the huge window above the altar and refused to let go of the sense of peace that was in him. She was unattainable, not just because she was Allie, but because he was promised to someone else. Simple facts of life both of them, unchangeable and therefore not worth fretting over.

She was with him now. That was all that mattered. And they were sharing this experience, something he could not imagine himself sharing with any other woman. Other women would prattle. She had said scarcely a word since they had entered the Abbey. She was his friend.

His soul mate. But he suppressed the thought. It could bring no peace at all, but only shatter it.

Her head was turned to him, and she was smiling when he looked at her next.

"I knew you would love it," she said, "even without your breakfast."

"And talking of breakfast," he said, reaching across and squeezing her clasped hands.

"There has been no internal orchestra to disturb other worshipers, after all," she said.

"Allie," he said as they got to their feet and made their way down the center aisle, "what an unladylike topic of conversation. I believe my stomach has been feeling the same sort of awe as the rest of me. Would you care to take breakfast at York House with me?"

"No," she said. "I have promised to go shopping with Andrea later this morning. And I fear it's already getting close to later this morning."

"Bonnets and slippers and feathers and such?" he said. "I would not dream of trying to interfere with such important feminine business. What does one do in the afternoons? Walk up to the Crescent? I am afraid these hills may be the end of me before I return to civilization. Though how I can look about me at these buildings and imply that I think Bath uncivilized escapes my understanding at present. What can I tempt you into doing this afternoon, Allie?" He closed his eyes briefly at his choice of words.

"How about Sidney Gardens?" she said. "It is very lovely, very fashionable, and very much at the bottom of the hill."

"Perfect," he said. "And so is the weather. I shall call for you after luncheon?"

"Yes," she said. "You do not need to escort me all the way home, you know, Piers. This is Bath and I am almost thirty years old."

"Are you really?" he said. "You are remarkably well preserved for one of such advanced years, I must say, Allie. Found the fountain of eternal youth, have you? And since when do you think I have lost all sense of chivalry and propriety that I would abandon you in the middle of a public street merely to scurry in pursuit of my breakfast?"

"It was just a thought," she said with a laugh. "I am used to being alone, Piers. I do not drag a maid about with me wherever I go."

"I am not a maid," he said. "Though the idea sets up a vastly amusing mental picture, does it not? Piers the plowman I have heard of and used my fists to defend myself against on more than one occasion at school. But Piers the maid? Would you force me to wear a mobcap?"

"With ribbons streaming down the back," she said. "I wish I had not tried to be kind and send you home for your breakfast. You are in one of your absurd moods, I see."

"And a feather duster?" he asked. "I could think of all sorts of interesting uses for a feather duster."

"But maids have to be demure," she said.

"The devil!" he said. "Do they? I have lost interest, then."

An afternoon strolling in Sidney Gardens, stopping several times—to exchange civilities with Colonel and Mrs. Smithers, with Mr. Horvath and Miss Druce, with other acquaintances. An evening taking tea at the Upper Assembly Rooms with the Wainwrights and the Potters. A morning at the Pump Room again, both of them tasting the waters merely to say they had done so, and grimacing at each other, and drinking valiantly on so that neither would be put to shame by the other. A stroll up to the Crescent in the afternoon, Piers pulling at Alice's arm and panting in great, wheezing gasps and declaring that he was sure he would not make it alive both there and back.

"But it will be all downhill on the way back," she said soothingly. "You can run all the way, Piers."

"And trip over my own feet very like and roll to the bottom with a broken crown like Jack," he said.

"But think of the view from the top," she said, laughing as he dragged more heavily than ever at her arm. "And the magnificence of the houses on the Crescent, Piers. And think of how fashionable a place it is to take a stroll and what a feather in one's cap to be seen walking there."

"I don't possess a cap," he said. "But if you say it is fashionable, Allie, then all that is important has been said. One would climb a hill twice as long and twice as steep in such a good cause."

There was no more pulling at her arm. Indeed, she was soon laughing at the necessity of keeping up to his pace.

An evening at the theater with the Potters, and supper at Sidney Place afterward. And talking until midnight.

"Quite a shocking hour to be up in Bath," Mr. Potter said as they rose to leave. "Even the balls here must end at eleven, Westhaven. Would you believe it? The focus of the whole city is on the waters, which must be taken early in the morning."

"Barbarous," Piers commented. "Do these people not know that civilized living ought not to start before noon or end before four in the morning? Good night, Allie. I will see you in the Pump Room in the morning?"

"Yes," she said. "Good night, Piers." And she turned to bid good night to her other friends.

Time was going altogether too fast. Too wonderfully and too fast. They neither of them cared what construction Alice's friends and acquaintances put on the fact that they spent so much of their days together. There was so little time left. Certainly no time to worry about what others would think.

Andrea was intrigued. She broached the subject when she and Alice were at the library together on the morning of the second day.

"Mr. Westhaven's betrothal is a recent event?" she asked.

"Yes," Alice said. "Since my own return from London."

Andrea frowned. "And was it an arranged thing?" she asked. "One of those matches planned from the girl's cradle on?"

"No," Alice said. "He met her just recently."

"But why?" Andrea asked. "Why, when you and he are so obviously head over ears in love, Alice?"

"Oh, that is not so." Alice was shaken from her calm. "You do not understand, Andrea. We have known each other all our lives, and very well since Web started to court me. We have shared each other's joys and sufferings—our marriages, my son's death and his wife's and child's, Web's passing. Friends grow very close under such circumstances. More like brother and sister than friends.''

"A very incestuous relationship for brother and sister, I would say," Andrea said with a smile.

Alice flushed.

"And I am not being much of a friend, am I?" Andrea said. "Goading you like this when you so clearly want to keep it all to yourself. It is just that I am fond of you, Alice. And you are far too young and far too pretty to have settled to this life you are living. I hoped when you went to London, even though you went merely to nurse your nephew and niece through the measles, that you would meet some gentleman more worthy of you than Sir Clayton. When Mr. Westhaven walked into your drawing room and almost into your arms, I thought it had happened."

"Well, it had not," Alice said with a smile. "And I do not need another marriage, Andrea. I have had the best one anyone could wish for in this life. I wish you had known Web. He was a wonderful person. And that is not just the opinion of a partial wife. Everyone who knew him loved him."

"I know," Andrea said. "I try to imagine how I would feel if I lost Clifford. I am sure I would feel as you do. But I am thirty-seven, Alice. You were twenty-seven when your husband died. So very young. Well, enjoy the rest of your friend's visit, my dear. I will not pry any further. Not until I can resist the temptation no longer, that is."

They both laughed.

But Alice refused to allow her mind to be disturbed by the knowledge that her friends were indeed misconstruing the situation and imagining that she and Piers were in love. Let them think it. It was the simple truth in her case, and she could not feel shame at loving another woman's betrothed. She did not care. For these few days she did not care.

But the morning after the visit to the theater she did not keep her appointment to meet Piers in the Pump Room. That was the morning when the sun was shin-

ing through the curtains in her room again, and full of
the joys of spring and the anticipation of another day
with him, she threw back the bedclothes and jumped
out of bed. And immediately had to clutch the bed-
post. And made it to the washstand only just in time
to save herself from vomiting all over the floor.

She stood holding firmly to the marble top of the
washstand, her head bowed forward, her eyes closed,
concentrating on not fainting away. Her face felt cold
and clammy. The air was cold in her nostrils.

She felt strangely calm. She had suspected it for a
few days, of course. She was never later than two or
three days at the most. It had already been five days.
She had known. Her subconscious mind had already
started to grapple with the truth and all its implica-
tions.

She had not begun to suspect with Nicholas. The
morning vomiting had been the first sign then. It had
continued unabated for two months, until poor Web
had been distraught and miserable with remorse for
having impregnated her.

She was with child again. There was no doubt in her
mind. And no panic. There was no definite thought at
all, except the sure knowledge.

She was with child. There was the beginnings of a
child inside her. Hers. And Piers'. She was going to
have Piers' child. A part of him. It had not after all
been an isolated experience in the past, over and done
with and to be relived only in memory. It was continuing into the present and the future. She would carry
that experience with her for nine months, and then she
would have his child. Perhaps his son.

The panic would begin soon. The dreadful knowledge that what they had done would be evident for all
to see. The knowledge that she would bear a child out
of wedlock. The guilt. The remorse. The terror. They
would all begin soon.

This strange gladness, this elation, would not outlive the return of common sense and cold reality.

She was not going to faint. And she did not think

she would vomit again. She groped her way back to
the bed and lay on her side. She pulled the covers up
over her ears. She lay there shivering and frightened.
And buried her face in the pillow, smiling with the joy
of it all.

She had Piers' child inside her. Now. At this very
moment. She spread a hand over her abdomen and
closed her eyes very tightly.

Piers had stayed at the Pump Room for an hour,
talking with the Wainwrights and Miss Dean, and with
the Potters when they arrived rather late. When it was
evident that Alice was not coming, and Mr. Potter was
engrossed in a lively discussion with Mr. Wainwright,
he offered his arm to Andrea Potter and strolled about
the room with her.

"Midnight must be too late an hour for Allie to be
up," he said. "I shall have to tease her about not
being able to get out of bed this morning."

"Alice is always up early," she said. "There must
be some domestic crisis that needs her attention. She
brought a young groom from London last week, and
then the housekeeper complained that Alice's maid was
daydreaming all day long."

"Ah," he said, "the course of true love not running
smooth again?"

"Apparently not," she said. "And you, sir—you
have just become betrothed?"

"And am to be married before the summer is out,"
he said, "if my betrothed can just complete the essen-
tial task of gathering all her bride clothes before then.
That is exclusively feminine business, I gather. My
presence in London was not in any way necessary this
week."

"I see," she said. "So you came to visit your old
friend. We are all delighted you did, sir."

"Are you?" he said, pursing his lips in some
amusement. "And are like to tie your tongue in knots,
ma'am, trying to ask the unaskable."

"Oh," she said, flushing and looking up at him, "how mortifying. Am I so transparent, sir?"

"On this particular topic, yes," he said. "We are just dear friends, I assure you. If you had known her husband, you would understand why she would never afford me a second glance in that particular way. He had everything to offer a woman of Allie's nature— kindness and steadiness of character. I could make the list longer."

"But there is no reason why *you* would not afford *her* a second glance?" she asked.

"You are very perceptive," he said. "Who could know Allie and not love her? But my life has been neither spotless nor productive, ma'am. Even if I loved her in that particular way and felt so inclined, I would have nothing of value to offer her, except money and property and a title perhaps long in the future. Can you see Allie being tempted by such lures?"

"No," she said. "You are very different from what I have thought in the past few days."

"Assume the question asked," he said. "I am, of course, a curious fellow."

"You seemed at first acquaintance to have a great deal of self-confidence," she said. "I would have expected that you would have a good image of yourself."

"Now why," he said, "do I have the impression that my soul is being laid out like an unrolled parchment and carefully scrutinized?"

"I do beg your pardon," she said. "I am not usually so unmannerly. I am just rather fond of Alice, that is all. Will you come home to breakfast with us? I promised to drag Alice off shopping afterward. Perhaps you would care to come, too."

"It sounds like an attractively devious plan," he said. "I accept. This is my last day here, you know. Do you think perhaps she is avoiding me by design?"

"I have very strong doubts," she said.

"But good-byes are hard to say," he said, "when a friendship is a very close one."

"Yes," she said. "Even when friendship is all, good-byes are hard."

He looked at her sidelong. "Do you make a specialty of tripping up people conversationally?" he asked. "I am not going to say it aloud, you know. You must guess at it if you will, and torture yourself with the possibility that you may be wrong."

"Ah," she said with a sigh, smiling rather roguishly at him, "I am almost certain that I am not. But you are right. There is always the niggling doubt. You are quite as reticent as Alice."

But what kept Allie? he wondered as they strolled on and rejoined Mrs. Potter's husband and the Wainwrights. She had been quite definite about coming this morning. And he had detected no reluctance in her during the past two days to spending her time with him. Had she indeed overslept? Had he outstayed his welcome? Had something kept her? Was she unwell?

They had only one day left. He had decided to return to London the next day.

A late morning visit to the shops on Milsom Street and tea and cakes at a confectioner's, when Andrea Potter suddenly remembered that she had business to conduct elsewhere for her husband and must leave them alone. Alice would not eat any cakes, but merely sipped tea, which she drank without milk. And she smiled at his teasing and looked at him with wide and luminous eyes, but would not participate as she usually did.

An afternoon strolling in Sidney Gardens again. They had the place almost to themselves since it was a cold and blustery day. But rain drove them out of there and home long before—hours, days before—they were ready to go of their own accord.

An evening of playing cards at the colonel's. And an early night.

A frustrating and a disappointing day. Over far too soon. And all over now, except for the good-byes in the morning.

Just a few weeks before, he would have invited himself inside for a comfortable sit and talk before taking himself back to his hotel. But not any longer. The most he could allow himself was a few minutes in his carriage before helping her down and watching her disappear inside her house.

"You are sure it was just tiredness this morning, Allie?" he asked. "You looked quite pale when I arrived with Mrs. Potter."

"The last few days have been busy ones," she said with a smile. "I do not usually venture out morning, afternoon, and evening, you know. And last night was rather late. I am afraid I just could not force myself to get up when the time came. I am sorry now. I missed an hour of your company."

"A dreadful thing to miss," he said. "Your life will be forever impoverished, Allie."

But she would not pick up his tone. "I am sorry all the same," she said. "And that it rained this afternoon. I could have wished that today would be perfect."

"Will you be at the Pump Room tomorrow morning?" he asked.

She shook her head. "No," she said. "No, I won't."

He looked at her in the darkness of the carriage for a few silent moments. "Does that mean you do not want to see me tomorrow?" he asked. "I plan to leave before noon."

"No," she said softly. "I did not mean that, Piers."

"I shall call here tomorrow then on my way out?" he asked.

"Yes." She nodded.

And there was nothing more to say. They sat and gazed at each other from opposite corners of the carriage and could not even smile.

"Well," he said softly.

"Well," she said.

He tapped on the panel, and his coachman set down the steps. As a final touch, Piers noticed, the rain had started again. All he could do was hand her down from the carriage and hurry her up the steps to the house.

"Good night," he said.

"Good night, Piers."

And she was gone.

He would see her for perhaps five minutes the next morning, when he would be tongue-tied with all there was to say. And then the journey back to London. And Cassandra. And his wedding. And the rest of his life.

And never Allie again.

Never again.

He clenched his hand into a fist suddenly and pounded the side of it lightly and rhythmically against the side of the carriage. He clenched his teeth hard. Devil take it, he was not about to cry, was he? With the whole wide lobby of York House to walk through before he could reach the privacy of his own rooms?

The last time he had cried was when he had held Allie in his arms after Web died.

God!

# 15

ALICE deliberately got up early the following morning so that she would be feeling more herself later. She hoped and she dreaded as she got gingerly out of bed that she would not have to go through the nausea and dizziness again that morning and each day for the next two months or so. But any fear—or should it be hope?—that her indisposition of the morning before had had another cause was soon put to rest.

She was still not feeling quite the thing when Piers arrived to take his leave of her, but she was dressed in her smartest morning dress and had had Penelope dress her hair in its most becoming style. And she was smiling.

"Piers," she said when he was shown into the drawing room, "you are on your way. You have a better day for travel than yesterday would have been."

"Yes," he said. "Altogether too good to be cooped up inside a carriage, by the look of it. Perhaps I will squeeze up onto the seat between Maurice and Joe. Or send Joe to sit inside. I am sure he would enjoy the sleep."

"Joe is not your coachman, by any chance, is he?" she asked.

"The very fellow," he said with a grin. "Well, Allie."

"Well, Piers." She smiled at him, her hands clasped loosely before her. "Have a safe journey."

"Yes." He set his head to one side and looked at her closely. "Why so pale? Are you unwell?"

"Yes, decidedly," she said, the smile even wider.

"I hate saying good-bye to those I am fond of, Piers. I wish you were in London already and this all over with. Do you know what I mean?"

He nodded.

"I am glad you came, though," she said. "Very glad that we are friends again."

"Yes." He extended a hand to her and she took it after a moment's hesitation. "I am deeply sorry about that other, Allie. We must put it behind us as if it had never been. Take care of yourself."

"Yes," she said. "And you."

So much to say. And nothing at all to say. She quelled her panic and concentrated on breathing slowly and evenly. She smiled. She thought every bone in her hand would break.

"Allie," he said. "Let me hug you."

And she was in his arms, her head pillowed against his shoulder, held to him, rocked against him. She closed her eyes and willed herself to remember every detail of this moment for the rest of her life. The hard muscularity of his body. The comfort of his arms and his shoulder. His cheek against the top of her head. The warmth and the smell of him. He and she, and their child between them.

Perhaps thirty seconds. At the most a minute. A minute to last a lifetime.

"There." He was grinning down at her. "Do you have a bone in your body that is not broken, Allie? If not, I shall do it again."

"As soon as you let me go," she said, "I shall crumple in a heap to the floor."

"Swooning at my feet?" he said. "How very flattering. Let us put this to the test, shall we?" He released his hold on her. "Ah, you lied, Allie."

"At this last possible moment you have discovered my great vice," she said. "On your way, sir, before you discover more."

"That is a tempting idea," he said. "But I have horses waiting, alas. And Maurice and Joe. Good-bye, Allie."

"Good-bye, Piers," she said.

They smiled cheerfully at each other for a few moments longer before he turned sharply and strode from the room.

Alice continued to smile at the door, her chin raised, her hands clasped tightly before her until she could no longer hear the sound of his horses clopping off into the distance. Then she sat down on the nearest chair and dropped her head as low as it could go.

The secret was to keep busy. To bath and change his clothes as soon as he arrived back at his rooms in London and go to White's Club to find diversion. To find friends and acquaintances and even enemies if necessary.

Gambling had never held out any lures for him. But on the night of his return he played cards almost until dawn and came away with six hundred more pounds in his pockets than he had had when he started. Drinking had never been one of his vices, but that night he drank himself drunk and then sober again. Apart from a headache and a foul mood, he felt no different when he left the club than he had when he went in.

He had not whored for years, having given it up as a somewhat nauseating and unhealthy excess of youth. And yet he found himself at dawn in the frilled boudoir and perfumed bed of a skilled courtesan who had been his mistress for a spell years before. But he could not remember when he awoke considerably later in the morning, his head on her ample bosom, if he had done more than sleep.

She neither complained nor looked contemptuous, so he concluded that his behavior had been entirely normal. But she smiled at him, clearly expecting something in return for providing his head with a pillow until such a late hour of the morning.

"Well, Sal," he said. "Have I been sleeping and wasting all this delicious softness?"

"That you have," she said. "But it's still available to you. For old times' sake. You always was the best."

"Ah, for old times' sake, then," he said, turning her beneath him and waiting for her to accommodate herself to him before lowering his weight. "Let me see if I can live up to my reputation, Sal."

He almost could not. He almost compared her to another woman. But he closed his eyes tightly and buried his nose in the harsh, sweet perfume of Sally's hair and drove himself toward forgetfulness and release.

"Ooh," she said, sighing with satisfaction a few minutes later, "I'll have bruises to remember this one by."

"I'm sorry, Sal," he said, kissing her and rolling away. He sat on the edge of the bed, his aching head in his hands for a few moments. "Deuce take it, I wish I were dead."

She chuckled throatily. "You'll take the rest of the day to sleep this one off," she said. "How much did you drink, anyway?"

"The sea dry," he said, getting resolutely to his feet and beginning to pull his clothes on.

Ten minutes later Sally was gaping and planning her retirement from a profession that was only very occasionally satisfying—as it had been all too briefly that morning. She was counting out the money Mr. Westhaven had left on the table by the door of her boudoir, and recounting it very slowly and carefully with trembling hands.

Six hundred pounds in addition to double her usual fee.

Alice waited until the next day before calling on Andrea to tell her that she had received a letter from Web's cousin and his family in Yorkshire, inviting her to stay with them for the summer. Indeed, they even wished her to live with them indefinitely, but she was not sure yet that she wished to commit herself to such an arrangement.

"You are going away again so soon and for such a long time?" Andrea asked in dismay. "Oh, Alice, and I have so enjoyed having you back here again. I did not know your husband had any living relatives except the ones who inherited your home.''

''They are on his mother's side,'' she said. ''Web was always close to them, but they have been traveling for the last year and more. Now they are home to stay.''

Andrea clucked her tongue. ''Well,'' she said, ''it is very selfish of me to wish you were not going, Alice. But surely you cannot seriously be considering staying there to live? You seem to value your independence so highly.''

''But it is hard to be alone,'' Alice said. ''I still miss Web, Andrea. Sometimes almost more than I can bear. Oh, how foolish of me.'' She rose sharply to her feet and crossed the room to the window.

And how hypocritical! She had spent the whole of the day before in a nightmare of longing for Web's friend. She was carrying the child of Web's friend. And yet, and yet it was true. The night before she had hugged her pillow against her and stretched her arm out to the side of the bed where Web had always lain and longed and longed for the safe comfort of his presence again. If only he had not died, if only he had not been so foolish and laughed at her scoldings and pleadings that he not go out in the rain before he was quite recovered from his illness. He had kissed her and called her a mother hen and told her that if she really insisted, he would stay and hold her hand all day and read with her.

She had not insisted.

If only she had. If only he were still alive. She would have been saved from all the temptation, all the turmoil. For if Web were alive, she would not have dreamed of dragging her feelings for Piers up beyond the realm of dreams. All that had happened would not have happened. She would not be raw with pain. She would be safely content.

And now she was crying for Web, noisily and awkwardly gulping back her sobs for him. Dear, safe Web, whose arm could be comfortingly about her now, on whose shoulder her head could be nestling. Toward whose happiness all her energies could be devoted, as they had been for nine years.

"I loved him, Andrea," she said. "I did love him."

"I do not doubt it for a moment," her friend said from behind her, her voice distressed. "No one is arguing with you, Alice. And do you feel guilty now for loving his friend?"

"I always have," Alice said quietly after drying her eyes and blowing her nose. She was still facing toward the window. "Since before I married Web. Since I was fourteen years old and he was handsome, devil-may-care, charming, one-and-twenty years old, and as far beyond me as the northern star. But I did love Web, too. He was the dearest man I have ever known. I would not have married him if I had been unable to love him."

"Well," Andrea said briskly, "a confession when I had given up trying to extract one. And the whole mystery of why Mr. Westhaven is not now marrying you instead of the girl in London—I do not even know her name. But I can understand your need to get away for a while. New scenery and new faces may be just what you need. Don't stay, though, Alice. You would not be happy living with someone else's family. Now turn around. Let me see how red your eyes are. A good brisk walk around to the Crescent is what you need, my girl, and perhaps a march down to the shops. I dare you to buy the bonnet you have been resisting for the last three days."

Alice laughed shakily and turned around.

"Hm," Andrea said. "Nothing that a little cold water will not disguise. Come to my dressing room with me. Perhaps we will meet a handsome stranger on Milsom Street. If so, I shall drop my reticule at his feet and effect an introduction. And you will be bowled off your feet and forget your Mr. Westhaven in the snap of a finger."

Alice laughed. "He must be worth ten thousand a year at least," she said.

"Done," Andrea agreed. "It will be the first question I ask when he picks up my reticule."

Two days later Alice left, completely alone, for Devonshire. She traveled post. There was a remote village close to the sea, where she and Web had spent a day during their wedding journey. They had wandered hand in hand along the beach on a sunny, blustery day, laughing with the effort of keeping their hats from blowing away, marveling at the sunlight dancing on the waves.

"If I ever had to leave Chandlos, Allie," he had said, "if I were ever wanted by the law for some grand crime of passion, I think I would come here. I think I could live contentedly here for a lifetime. With you beside me, of course."

He had kissed her there on the deserted beach. She could still remember the newness of being able to allow such liberties, her relief at finding that she liked Web to touch her. She had always enjoyed intimacy with him, enjoyed the evidence of his pleasure.

She did not know why she remembered that particular place and those particular words. But she did. And she had decided almost immediately that she would go there. There was a good posting inn close by, where she and Web had stayed. She would stay there for a day or two and inquire about the availability of cottages in the area. She would stay there for a few months if she could while she made a more final decision about her future and her child's.

At the inn where she spent the first night, she packed away the clothes she had worn that day at the bottom of a trunk of black garments. If within a few months she was to be noticeably a woman with child, then she must be recently widowed.

She felt a pang of guilt toward a husband who had died and been bitterly mourned more than two years before.

A long soak in a hot bath to rid himself of Sally's perfume and the whole debauch of the night and morning, and two cups of strong black coffee made Piers feel at least human again, even if they did not rid him of his headache or the knowledge that he had reacted to pain and loss in a remarkably immature manner— as usual. Nothing much ever changed in his life, except the incidentals.

It would have felt good to follow Sally's advice and sleep for the rest of the day. But sleeping would not cure him of a hangover, as he knew from experience. He dressed in his most fashionable London finery, put on his best expression of careless dandyism, and set forth in the direction of Russell Square.

By some miracle Cassandra was at home with her mother, though she was to drive out to St. James's Park later—with Sir Clayton Lansing, of all people. Piers was only thankful that the gentleman had not taken himself off back to Bath to bother Allie again.

"Ah, my dear," he said after exchanging civilities with Lady Margam. "How lovely it is to see you again. And in better looks than ever." He took Cassandra's hand and raised it to his lips.

It was true, too. Someone had clearly advised her that a young lady about to become a young matron should rid herself of some of her ringlets. Her hair was shorter, less fussy, far more becoming.

"I have been busy," she said, "and out every day and every evening. Have I not, Mama?"

"I do not doubt it," he said, smiling down at her. "I shall have to keep a jealous eye on my betrothed, I can see, or she will be snatched from under my nose."

"I do not like jealousy," she said. "We will have to come to an agreement before our marriage on the amount of freedom each of us will be allowed."

"Ah," he said, raising his eyebrows and pursing his lips. "But freedom to do what, pray?"

"To be admired by others," she said. "To spend time with others. You are not planning to be Gothic, are you, sir?"

"My love," her mother admonished quietly.

"I don't believe it will be within my power," he said. "I do not have any cobwebby attics or haunted garrets to lock you inside at Westhaven. You may rest easy, Cassandra."

"Whatever are you talking about?" she asked, looking bewildered and not a little impatient. "Mama and I have drawn up a list of wedding guests. You must look it over to see if you wish to add any names. There are four hundred and twelve at the moment."

"Good Lord," he said. "Do we know that many people?"

"We do not wish to give offense by omitting anyone," she said.

"Ah, of course," he said. "You have not forgotten the sweep who cleaned my chimneys last summer, have you, Cassandra? He will be ferociously wrathful if we forget him." He grinned at her.

"How foolish you can be," she said. "It has been hard work to draw up the list, has it not, Mama? It is certainly no joke."

"I do beg your pardon, my dear," he said, making her a bow. "If it pleases you to have four hundred guests at our wedding, then proceed. I am sure there is no one I would wish to add to the list."

"I have not included Mrs. Penhallow," she said. "She has gone home to Bath, has she not, and would be unlikely to return for the wedding. Doubtless she would not wish to be reminded of her own widowhood, anyway. It is a pity for her sake that she is not a few years younger. Perhaps she would be able to find herself another husband if she were. But gentlemen do not like their brides to be beyond the age of twenty, do they?"

"You have done the right thing," Piers said. "Mrs. Penhallow would not be interested in returning for our wedding."

"Well, then," she said, "I must get ready to drive with Sir Clayton, sir. He was very insistent and I did have this afternoon free. You may escort Mama and me to Lady Audley's concert this evening."

"Thank you," he said. "I shall look forward to it."

He did not know whether to laugh or rage as he drove away in his curricle ten minutes later. And he did not know whether he would take her over his knee the day after their wedding and give her a thorough walloping—it was almost a shame that he did not believe in wife beating—or give her the freedom she clearly desired and enjoy the greater freedom he would have as a result.

It was also something of a shame that he did not believe in marital infidelity—by either the husband or the wife. He really did not think he could tolerate his wife's lovers—and he had a strong premonition that they would be plural—calling at his house to take her driving in the park and on to their particular lovers' nest.

No, of course, he would not be able to take the easy and in some ways the most desirable course. He must gird his loins for the battle of a lifetime with his future wife.

Alice stayed away for three months. She was fortunate enough to find just what she was looking for: a cottage that had belonged to two sisters, until one of them had died and the other had moved away to live with a married brother. The cottage was for rent. It was situated at the edge of a village only a few miles from the one Alice had had in mind. It was almost within sight of the sea.

She hired a maid and a cook from the village and settled to a life of quiet domesticity. She made friends with the rector's wife and the local squire's family. But she was not expected to participate in all the social life of the neighborhood, being apparently a lady in deep mourning.

She had kept her own name. If she should decide that this was where she wished to settle for the rest of her life, she had thought at first, then this was where her child would grow up. She would not wish to complicate his life by giving him a false name.

She thought about her future and about her child's during endless walks along the cliffs and on the beach. Whatever happened, wherever she finally settled, she would tell the child the truth from the start. She would not tell anyone else. She would try at least to ensure that he was given a normal childhood, without the label of illegitimacy. But he must know that she had never been married to his father, and the sooner she told him, the better.

Whether she would also tell him who his father was, she had not decided even at the end of the three months. He would have the right to know, of course, but she hated the thought of his going to find his father when he was old enough to do so. It would be far better if Piers never knew. He would have his own family to concern himself with. And she certainly did not want him to feel obliged to find her out at that future date to make some sort of atonement.

No atonement was needed. She had had her night of love and had never regretted it, and she had been left with a priceless gift for a lifetime. At the end of the three months she was still waiting for the panic and the guilt to replace the elation. But as the signs of her pregnancy became more definite, she could only feel more deeply the warm gladness she had felt on that first morning.

Now it was even better. The morning nausea had stopped promptly at the end of the second month.

She was content where she was. She liked the thought of bringing up her child in that particular part of the world. Indeed, she would have been quite happy never to have to go back, to sever the ties with her past without any further effort. But there was a home in Bath to be sold and servants to be helped to other positions. There were possessions to be brought to Devonshire or otherwise disposed of. There were arrangements to be made about the house in London. There were a thousand other pieces of business to do.

And if she must go, she decided finally, then she should go without further delay. For in another month's time, perhaps sooner, her condition would be becoming obvious to other people, too. She would hate to put Andrea and her other friends in the awkward position of noticing and pretending not to do so, of wondering who the father was. Andrea would guess, of course.

She would go now, much as she dreaded the thought. If she worked hard, she could complete all her business in one week. Then she could come back and forget and be forgotten. She could begin her new life in earnest.

She returned to Bath late in August.

Those months for Piers were neither so tranquil nor so uneventful. He was soon caught up in the whirl of the second half of the Season by the necessity of taking his betrothed about whenever no other favored gentleman was taking his place.

Mr. Bosley had the marriage contract drawn up, he declared genially, but had forgotten it at his office one afternoon when Piers called at the house. A few days later he had noticed a minor clause that had been copied wrongly and would need a little rewriting. It would be ready within a couple more days.

Piers waited for his chance to have a talk with Cassandra. It was not easy, when very little of her time was free for her fiancé and almost none of that was private time. But they must talk, he had decided. It would not be fair to wait until after the wedding before making clear to her that he expected—and would demand—a wife who would be faithful to him in both fact and appearance, that he expected a wife who would be mistress of Westhaven and a mother to his children.

He would have to explain, of course, that he would be willing to give her pleasure, too, by taking her to London for the Season or to one of the spas for the summer months. He was prepared to give. But a marriage could not succeed on all giving, whoever was the giver. She must also be prepared to give. He must make that clear to her.

And all the time he worried about Alice. She had not been leading too busy a life in Bath. Allie was not a vaporish female. She had been sick, not tired on that morning when she had not come to the Pump Room. And she had refused to come there the following morning, though it was his last. Why? Because she had feared—or known—that she would be sick again?

She had looked very pale when he had gone to say good-bye to her. Why? Because he was leaving? But then his leaving would not have meant that much to her. She had merely been saying farewell to a friend. Had she been sick again?

For two mornings in a row?

God!

He never did have his talk with Cassandra, after all. He arrived at Russell Square one afternoon to take her to Madame Tussaud's to find Bosley alone in his drawing room, rubbing his hands together in apparent embarrassment. Cassandra, it seemed, had eloped that very morning with Sir Clayton Lansing, the naughty puss.

"I should cut her off without a penny," Bosley said. He shook his head. "But such is young love, and such is an uncle's fondness, sir, that she will doubtless succeed in wrapping me about her little finger again when she returns a married lady."

Piers clasped his hands behind his back and pursed his lips. He concentrated on not showing any outward signs of amusement. It would be inappropriate at the moment. Lansing and young love? Cassandra and *love?* Bosley being wrapped about anyone's little finger? It was all vastly diverting. He looked forward to telling Alice all about it.

But that thought sobered him in earnest.

"It is a good thing under the circumstances, my dear sir," Bosley was saying, "that the marriage contract has not been signed. You might have taken me

for my fortune if you had been an unscrupulous man."
He laughed heartily.

Well, Piers thought, if this was a stage, he could be
every bit as good an actor as Bosley, and probably
better. He could scarcely be worse. He delivered what
he considered an affecting speech of disappointment
and took his sober leave.

His mother did not seem greatly affected by his
news. "Good," she said. "Next time, Piers, perhaps
you will have the wisdom to choose someone closer to
your own age, and someone with your interests and
vastly more sense than you."

"I think I would prefer that there not be a next time,
Mama," he said, kissing her cheek as he took his leave
of her.

"Nonsense!" she said. "The lady for you is probably under your very nose, Piers. Besides, I was foolish enough to have no other children but you. You are
my only hope for grandchildren."

Piers was on his way to Westhaven Park two days
later, though he decided at the last moment to go to
Bath first. Just to let Allie know. Not for any other
reason. He must not conceive any hopes that he knew
in advance were totally unrealistic. But he would call
just to let her know. She would be glad for him. He
need not stay longer than one night.

Besides, there was something he needed to check
on for his own peace of mind.

# 16

"A COUSIN of Web's in Yorkshire." Piers frowned.

"On his mother's side," Andrea explained to him. "They were very close, she said, but the cousin and his family have been traveling for the past year. Now they are home, and they want Alice with them for the summer, and even longer than that, apparently."

Piers continued to frown at the floor in front of his feet.

"I thought she would write," Andrea said. "Though of course she still may do so. She has been gone for only a month."

"I shall go there," he said, getting to his feet in sudden decision.

"Yorkshire is rather a large part of the country to wander over," she said. "Do you know where to go?"

"I went there once with Web when we were young sprigs on our way to seek adventure in Scotland," he said. He grinned at her. "I shall tell Allie it is time she wrote to her friends."

Andrea returned his smile. "Perhaps she will return with you," she said. "Perhaps she will be in time to attend your wedding."

"Why did you not merely ask without roundaboutation?" he said, winking at her before turning toward the door. "There is to be no wedding, ma'am. The lady cried off in order to elope with an acquaintance of yours—Sir Clayton Lansing. Ah, something about young love, I believe. There is no stopping it, apparently."

"Oh." Andrea clasped her hands to her bosom and

watched his retreating back. "I love it. And where is Clifford when I most need him? I shall burst if I do not find someone within the hour with whom to share this delightful *on dit*. I shall not pretend to commiserate with you, sir."

"Thank you," he said.

The next morning, Piers left early for the long journey to Yorkshire, though he knew that he was on a wild goose chase. There was indeed a cousin in Yorkshire, a reclusive misogynist who had greeted Web and him coldly and offered them neither a meal nor a bed for the night. They had laughed about it for the rest of their journey through Scotland.

And Allie had gone there? If she had, she must have gone without an invitation and doubtless would not have been welcomed. And yet after a month she had not come home again. He was as sure as he could be that there were no other relatives in Yorkshire, certainly none to whom Web had been close.

Yet if she had not gone there, where had she gone? And why? Or if she had gone there without an invitation, why had she done so? And where had she gone after she had been turned away, as she surely would have been?

He feared that he knew the answers to some of his questions.

God! Allie! Why had she not told him?

The most foolish of all his questions. Of course she would not have told him.

But where was she? England was rather a large country to search, not to mention the possibilities of Wales, Scotland, and Ireland, and perhaps even France and the Continent, he thought in somewhat of a panic when he discovered a week later that indeed she was not with the cousin in Yorkshire, and had not been there at all.

Cavendish Square? Portman Square? But no, she would not go to London. Bruce's home in the country? No, her brother would be the last person she would turn to under almost any circumstance, certainly the particular one he imagined she was in.

There was only one hopeful sign. She had left her house in Bath open and functioning, with all the servants. Surely she must come back at some time if only to settle her affairs. He could only hope it would be soon. Surely she would not stay away for the full nine months and then return alone, as if from Yorkshire. Would she?

Surely she would not do that. No, Allie would not do that.

He spent the following two months moving restlessly back and forth between Westhaven Park and Bath, with one brief journey to London to instruct his man of business to call regularly at Cavendish Square just on the chance that she would go there.

He happened to be at Westhaven Park when a short letter arrived from Andrea Potter to say that Alice was back and planning to leave again within a week in order to make her permanent home with her husband's cousins in Yorkshire.

The following day he took his usual suite of rooms at the York House hotel.

It was strange that she had not wanted to come back, Alice thought, but that now she had, she felt reluctant to return to her seaside cottage. Perhaps it had something to do with the fact that it was late summer and the days were unusually sunny and warm. Or with the fact that she had established this home after leaving Chandlos and built up a circle of friends whose acquaintance she valued. Or with the fact that her home in Bath was filled with furnishings and possessions that had been with her during her marriage and before, and everything could not go with her to Devonshire. Or with the fact that Piers had been with her in Bath and the place was filled with memories of him.

However it was, she did not particularly like the thought of going back. Yet she knew she must, and soon. Even the temptation to linger for a few weeks or a month must be resisted. As it was, she had waited almost too long. Her first comment to Andrea three days before, after kissing her and greeting her, had been a laughing one about how well her cousin's cook had fed her in Yorkshire and how she must look to her figure when she returned.

Andrea, bless her heart, had shown remarkably little curiosity about her three months spent in Yorkshire. Alice had been prepared with a whole arsenal of lies, but it was a relief not to have to use many of them.

She had visited all her friends, including Sir Harold Dean, who had been ailing for a few weeks, and had attended the theater with the Potters and Mr. Horvath the evening before. But she had been busy most of the time' and thankful for the necessity of keeping herself so.

On the fourth morning after her return she had been to the Pump Room, drawn there more by the bright morning sunshine and the craving for exercise and company than because she had nothing else to do. But the rest of the morning had to be spent overseeing the packing of the trunks that were to accompany her. She was wearing her oldest morning dress. Her hair had come somewhat awry since its morning dressing.

It was Mr. Horvath, she thought, looking down at herself in some despair when her housekeeper announced that there was a gentleman belowstairs to see her. She had said the evening before that she might walk with him in Sidney Gardens for an hour during the afternoon if she could get all her packing done first. But why had he come during the morning?

She hesitated only long enough to decide that she would not return to her room to change her dress and recomb her hair. After all, he knew that she was in the middle of her packing.

She hoped it was Mr. Horvath. Her feet faltered on the stairs at the thought that perhaps it was someone else. Sir Clayton, for example. She had forgotten to ask Andrea if he was back from London, though it seemed strange that she had not seen him if he were. And no one had mentioned him to her.

She hoped it was not he. She entered the salon rather cautiously. And closed the door with a bang behind her and extended both hands.

"Piers!" she said. "What a delightful surprise! What on earth are you doing in Bath? I thought you would be on your wedding journey by now. But perhaps you are? Is Miss Borden—I mean, is Mrs. Westhaven—with you? Are congratulations now in order?"

"Am I permitted to answer your questions in reverse order?" he asked, taking her hands and squeezing them tightly before releasing them. "Yes, definitely. No, she is not. No, I am not." He was checking the answers off on his fingers. "And what was the first? Ah yes. Visiting you. You would never believe me if I said taking the waters, would you?"

"Not for a moment," she said, laughing. "But I have forgotten my questions, you provoking man."

"Congratulations are definitely in order, Allie," he said. "I have been jilted in favor of a gentleman who has more to offer than I in terms of future assets, it seems. And perhaps you should sit down while I break a particularly nasty piece of news to you."

"What?" she asked, continuing to smile, and not taking a seat.

"You have been jilted, too," he said. "Lansing has absconded with the fishy heiress."

"What?" she said. "Piers!"

"True," he said. "Do you need me to send for your smelling salts, Allie?"

"No," she said. "But if you had a feather, you could knock me down with it, Piers."

"A shocking humiliation, is it not?" he said. "What are we going to do about it, Allie? Marry each other as a consolation?"

"No, silly," she said. "Oh, Piers, have you really been released from that dreadful betrothal? I am so glad."

"So is my mother," he said. "She told me to go out and find myself someone more sensible."

"A very commendable idea," she said. "And have you started to do that, Piers?"

"Yes," he said.

She smiled. "How coincidental that you have come just this week," she said. "I have been away for three months, you know. No, I suppose you do not know. I have been in Yorkshire with Web's cousin and his family."

"Ah," he said. "With Oscar. Charming fellow." His brow furrowed in thought. "What is his wife's name?"

"Cecily," she said.

"Yes, of course," he said. "They have three children?"

"Four," she said. "Two sons and two daughters."

"Ah," he said. "Far more sensible than three and one. Or four and nothing, for that matter. You enjoyed yourself, then, Allie?"

"Yes," she said. "I am going back there next week. Indefinitely. They want me to live with them."

"Yes, I can imagine they would," he said. "They are enormously hospitable people. Web and I almost did not get to Scotland when we called on them. They wanted us to stay forever."

"Yes," she said. "I can believe it. You were not in the Pump Room this morning, Piers?"

"No," he said. "I was all tired out from the journey yesterday. I am very thankful to find you here at the end of it, though. I would have hated to make the trip for nothing."

"Yes," she said. "I am glad I did not miss you."

"Been romping with the mice in the attic, have you, Allie?" he asked. "You look charmingly rumpled."

"Oh." She could feel herself flush and had to concentrate on keeping her wide smile intact. "I have been directing the packing of my trunks. I am closing the house, you see, and putting it on the market."

"Ah," he said. "A good idea. Will you come driving with me this afternoon, Allie?"

"Oh," she said. "I am so sorry. I have half promised to walk in Sidney Gardens with Mr. Horvath. I did not know you were here, Piers."

"No matter," he said. "What about this evening?"

She grimaced. "I have promised Miss Dean that I will sit with her father and read to him while she takes tea at the Upper Rooms," she said. "He has been quite unwell."

"And will I be interrupting a tête-à-tête if I accompany you?" he asked. "It would be embarrassing to find myself a third party to a proposal of marriage or anything of that nature."

"Piers." She laughed. "How absurd you are. It will be a dreadfully dull evening for you."

"You must have changed, then," he said. "There must be more changes about you than just the disheveled appearance. I have never found your company dull before, Allie."

"Come, then," she said. "But don't be surprised if Sir Harold nods off to sleep just when you are in the middle of what you think to be a particularly fascinating anecdote."

"Good Lord," he said. "Does he do that? I shall be sure to waste none of my best stories on him, then. But he sounds like the ideal chaperon, Allie. A rakish gentleman's dream come true. Unless he makes a habit of waking up at the wrong moments, that is."

She laughed again.

"I shall allow you to return to your trunks and your mice in the attic, then," he said. "One hates to interrupt a lady when she is having fun. I shall take you up in my carriage this evening, Allie, and hope fervently that Miss Dean does not neglect to give her father his sleeping draft before taking herself off in pursuit of tea."

He made her a half bow and held the door open for her to precede him into the hallway. His mouth was pursed in that way he had always had when he was entertaining some private and amusing thought about someone else.

Alice made her way upstairs and into the drawing room, where she sat down, glad of the privacy that she would not have had in her room, where both Penelope and her housekeeper were busy packing. Her legs were shaking, she noticed with some surprise as she took her weight off them.

Piers was the last person she had expected to see. She had thought never to see him again. And he was unmarried, unbetrothed, unattached.

She wished and wished that he had not come. She had thought all that turmoil behind her. She had achieved a hard-won measure of tranquillity in the past three months. She did not want it all destroyed. She did not want another few days with him. And then the inevitable parting again.

She did not believe she could hold on to her sanity if she had to go through all that again.

*If!* She was already going through it. She was already wishing poor Mr. Horvath a million miles away, and already wondering if she could squeeze all her business into a few hours a day so that she would have time to spend with Piers.

She did not want it. She did not want all this again. How she wished he had not come. What a cruel fate that he had chosen this of all weeks during which to pay her a call.

Web's cousin was Oscar. She had forgotten that. What a blessing that Piers had mentioned the name first. She had been planning to call him Claude. She hoped Piers would not remember the real name of the wife. She had felt a moment of panic when she had realized that he knew of the Yorkshire cousin. She must steer the conversation away from that particular topic during the evening.

She looked down at the faded blue of her muslin dress and raised her hands to her hair. Oh, what a mess she was. How dreadful she must look. How ob-

noxious and how typical of Piers to give her no warn-
ing that he was coming.

Allie was always impeccably neat and elegant, Piers
thought as he rode out into the hills beyond Bath that
afternoon. He could not remember seeing her before
that morning with even a hair out of place. Except for
one occasion, he supposed.

She had looked knee-weakeningly beautiful that
morning, faded old dress, untidy hair, smudged cheek,
and all. Of course there was that new fullness about
her face and breasts that perhaps would detract from
her beauty to an impartial observer. But on him they
had quite the opposite effect.

Oh, quite the opposite!

And so, he thought, dragging his mind free of his
own selfish elation, he had destroyed her after all. One
night of indiscretion on both their parts and the whole
of her life had been thrown into turmoil. Destroyed.

She would not now lose all her respectability, of
course, as she would have done if Bosley had been a
little more the gentleman and refrained from persuad-
ing Cassandra into eloping with Lansing. Despite the
sunshine and the warmth of the day, he turned cold at
the thought that he might have been married when he
discovered the truth. If he ever had discovered it for
certain.

But respectability was not all. Retaining it would
bring her no happiness. For retaining it would involve
marrying him. Allie was going to have to marry him.

Allie! The rector's daughter with her young woman's
slender body and large, calm eyes and silky dark hair.
The quiet girl turned woman, whom he had loved at a
glance when the transformation was effected. And
whom he had known himself unworthy of at the self-
same moment, for his youth had been marred by a
wild debauchery that had even come near to putting a
strain on his friendship with Web.

Allie. Web's betrothed. Web's bride. With the blushing cheeks and the luminous eyes, gazing at her bride-

groom with a virgin's wonder and timidity. Web's wife.
Serene and charming and gentle. A woman fulfilled.
A woman in love.

And Allie limp and silent in his arms while he wept,
numbed by her grief after Web died.

Allie, always beyond him, always worshiped, always
loved from afar, even when he had suppressed the
knowledge for a few years. And now, in one night of
folly he had defiled her and left the mark of his possession on her. She would have to marry him.

There was no cause for elation in the thought. Any
joy he had felt that morning as soon as he had set eyes
on her and known beyond any shadow of doubt was a
misplaced joy. Because it was for himself and not for
the woman he would have died for sooner than trap
into a joyless future.

But it must be done. He had no choices. And neither
had she.

Time was going too fast and too slowly again, Alice
thought later that evening during the carriage ride
home. She wanted it over, over and done with. She
wanted herself back in Devonshire, safe in her cottage, Bath and these days long behind her. And yet the
evening was gone already. And she had only three
more days until her planned journey. Piers had not
said how long he was to stay.

So little time. And all the pain looming ahead again.

"To be mistaken for Lansing!" Piers said beside
her. "The worst humiliation of my life, Allie."

She laughed. "Poor Sir Harold," she said. "He was
wandering in his mind even worse than when I saw
him two days ago. But he did add that he had forgotten
Sir Clayton was such a handsome devil, as he put it.
There is your consolation, Piers."

"Hm," he said. "And I thought he was supposed
to pop off to sleep, Allie. I left all my best stories at
York House and had to listen instead to the reminis-
cences of almost eighty years of living."

"You are wonderful with the elderly, Piers," she

said. "You need not pretend that you did not deliberately set out to give Sir Harold his happiest evening in a long while. Most people are impatient with his ramblings. You put on a great show of interest. And I do not believe for one moment that it really was all show."

"Ah," he said. "I did not have a moment for conversation with you, though, Allie."

"I shall be at the Pump Room tomorrow morning," she said with a smile as the carriage drew to a halt outside her house.

"I am going to invite myself in now," he said. "Will your housekeeper have a fit of the vapors, do you suppose?"

"No," she said after a moment's hesitation. "It is still quite early."

"Yes," he said, getting out of the carriage and turning to help her to the pavement. "And even if it were not, Allie."

She preceded him up the steps and did not stop to try to interpret his strange words. She was concentrating on keeping her breathing even. She was concentrating on smiling.

"Shall I have tea brought in?" she asked when they entered the drawing room. "Or chocolate? Or something stronger, perhaps?"

"Nothing," he said. He had crossed the room to the fireplace and stood with his elbow propped on the mantel. "Where have you been, Allie?"

"Been?" She frowned.

"When you were supposedly with Oscar and the mythical wife and four children," he said. "Where were you?"

She flushed. "I do not understand your meaning," she said.

"I met Oscar years ago," he said. "With Web. He would not have let you over the threshold, Allie. But to be doubly sure, I went there to see. Two months ago."

She stared at him. He did not look like Piers. All the humor was gone from his face.

"Where were you?"

She did not answer for a while. "Somewhere else," she said. "I do not have to explain myself to you, Piers."

"Maybe you will have to soon," he said. "You had better marry me, Allie."

"Don't be foolish," she said. She wished she had sat down when she came into the room. Now she felt stranded in the middle of the floor.

He looked at her for a long moment in silence. "We both know it is not foolishness," he said.

"What do you mean?" She felt horribly out of control of the conversation.

"You have seen yourself in the mirror every day," he said. "You would not have noticed changes. I have not seen you for three months."

She shook her head.

"You are not going to deny it, are you, Allie?"

"You are talking nonsense," she said.

"Am I?" He pushed himself away from the mantel and came purposefully toward her. She resisted the urge to turn and run.

He took her by the shoulders when he came up to her and turned her away from him. He drew her back against him. She closed her eyes and bit down hard on her upper lip as he spread both hands beneath her breasts and moved them slowly down her body. She rested her head back against his shoulder.

"You must be very thankful for this modern fashion of gowns that fall loose from beneath the bosom," he said. "They hide the loss of a waistline quite admirably."

She said nothing. What was there to say?

"So, Allie." He kept his hands spread on her. He spoke into her ear. "You had better marry me."

"No," she said. "Never." She pushed herself away from him. "Go away, Piers. Please go away."

"And let my child be born a bastard?" he said.

"And let him have Web's name? No, not that, Allie. Web always had everything I most wanted. And though I always envied him, I was never jealous, for he deserved everything he had a thousand times more than I would have done. But I will not allow him to have my child. *Our* child. Don't expect that of me."

"You don't have to take responsibility," she cried, whirling on him. "And you don't have to feel this terrible male need to protect. You don't have to, Piers. Because to me there is no disaster. I want this child. I could not possibly want anything more. In three months I have not been able to feel any guilt or any panic. And it does not matter that he will have Web's name. For he will always know that he is yours. And I will know that he is yours. I would not wish it otherwise if I could."

"Allie." He reached out to wipe a tear from her cheek that she had not even realized was there. "I wish it could be made otherwise. I wish for your sake it could be Web's. I wish I could bring him back for you and change this whole situation."

"Ohh!" she said. "Piers! Are you blind? Can't you see? Have you been blind all these years? Haven't you known that it has always been you? Always? From the time I was fourteen and in braids?"

She whisked herself over to a sofa and sat down on it. She rested her elbows on her knees and covered her face with her hands. And began to tremble. Had he left the room? Why the silence?

"So," he said finally. His voice sounded quite unlike itself. "You can have no objection to marrying me, then, Allie."

"I will not marry you just because you have got me with child, Piers," she said wearily into her hands.

"It seems we have been sharing a mutual blindness," he said very quietly. It sounded as if he were much closer.

She looked up sharply. He was stooped down on his haunches in front of her.

He looked into her eyes and nodded his head. "Not

quite so soon, though," he said. "I had to wait for the braids to disappear and some shape to blossom. You were fifteen."

She lost sight of him after a few more silent moments. She was biting hard on her upper lip again.

"Allie," he said. "A fifteen-year blindness. Suddenly ended. The light is dazzling, is it not?"

She nodded.

"I fell in love with you when I saw you that summer," he said. "I adored you for years afterward. You were so lovely, so pure, so totally unattainable. I married Harriet to try to forget you. I finally convinced even myself that I had done so. I convinced myself that you were just the dearest friend a man has ever had. Until that night in London, Allie. Blinding sight restored."

"You seemed so far beyond me," she said. "You were twenty-one, dashing, and handsome, and I just fourteen. I loved you passionately. I always dreamed of your loving me, far back where dreams are kept, though I loved Web with all the reality of everyday living. I have never stopped loving you, Piers, and I have never been able to regret what happened that night. Or its consequences. It was the most beautiful night of my life."

"Well," he said, running a knuckle lightly along her jawline. "Well."

They smiled tentatively at each other in the silence that followed.

"Allie," he said, "we must offer a prayer for Cassandra's and Lansing's happiness. And don't smile, wicked woman. I am in deadly earnest. I might not be here now—I would not be here now—if they had not decided to elope."

"No." Her smile faded.

He reached out a hand to put a lock of hair behind her ear. "Is this what pregnancy does to you?" he asked. "I have never known you as untidy as you have been today, Allie."

"Oh," she said.

"Very eloquent," he said. "Or so beautiful, I should add, just in case I have given the wrong impression. If pregnancy makes you beautiful, I shall have to keep you beautiful for the next ten years or so, shan't I?"

"Oh, Piers," she said shakily, "I feel dumb and stupid. I cannot think of any witty reply."

"I shall allow you six months to recover your wits," he said, framing her face with his hands and stroking his thumbs gently over her cheeks as he kissed her softly on the lips, parting his own. "And then give you a year or so before I set about making you beautiful and witless again."

"Piers!" She laughed shakily. "You are supposed to tell me that I am always beautiful."

"The devil! Am I?" he said. "I shall do so, then, Allie. On one condition."

She looked at him inquiringly.

"That first you tell me both that you love me and that you will marry me," he said.

"I love you." She moved forward so that her forehead touched his. "And I will marry you, Piers."

"In that case you are beautiful," he said. "Always so beautiful. And will be when you are nine and a half months huge with our child and when you are eighty years old. And I love you, Alice Penhallow. Alice Westhaven. Since you have forced my hand, I will marry you, too, you see."

She smiled.

"Now," he said, "two things to be done before I take myself off out of here and save your housekeeper from the vapors. A lengthy and lascivious and quite out-of-control kiss. And comfort from a mother-to-be to the terrified expectant father. Which should we put first?"

"Oh, Piers," she said, putting her arms about his neck, "don't be afraid. When I had Nicholas, the doctor told me I was one of those fortunate women who have babies so easily that it is almost not fair to the others. Don't be afraid. I am not. I have been so ex-

cited for three months that I have scarce known how
to contain my joy. Be excited with me for six more.''

"Well, if it's excitement you are asking for, Allie,''
he said, getting to his feet and holding to her elbows
so that she was forced up with him, ''we might as well
proceed to the second matter of business. Lengthy, I
said, did I not?'' He wrapped his arms about her and
kissed her lingeringly, his tongue tracing slowly the
line of her lips, before drawing back his head to smile
at her.

"And lascivious,'' she said, threading her fingers
through his hair and bringing herself full against him.
''I like that part, Piers.''

"Do you?'' he said. ''Shameless woman. And out
of control. That is the part I like best.''

"Me too,'' she said against his mouth.

"We had better get started, then,'' he said, ''or that
poor woman is going to be in a senseless heap on the
floor outside before we reach the end.''

"Mm,'' she said while she still could, ''are we going to reach the end, Piers?''

"Never,'' he said. ''I lied. I sometimes do, Allie.
Never the end, my love. Not now that I have you at
last. Only beginnings. Like this, you see.''

He opened his mouth over hers.